Paws and Punishment – A Norwegian Forest Cat Café Cozy Mystery – Book 5

By

Jinty James

Paws and Punishment – A Norwegian
Forest Cat Café Cozy Mystery – Book 5

By

Jinty James

Copyright © 2020 by Jinty James

DEDICATION

To Annie and AJ.

CHAPTER 1

Snip, snip, sni—

"Oops," Zoe muttered.

"Oops?" Lauren Crenshaw stared at her cousin in the bathroom mirror. Zoe's brunette pixie-cut stood up in angsty little tufts. "What do you mean, 'Oops'?"

"Brrt?" Annie, Lauren's Norwegian Forest Cat, asked as well. The large silver-gray tabby peered at both of them inquisitively as she sat on the edge of the tub.

"It's nothing to worry about," Zoe said, her brown-eyed gaze meeting Lauren's in the mirror. Doubt flickered in her eyes, but then she pinned a smile on her face. "I watched a video online about how to cut hair. I'm sure it will turn out just fine."

"What have you done?" Lauren felt the back of her head, her fingers searching for the freshly cut locks. She sucked in a breath, her eyes widening.

"I just took off a little more than I thought," Zoe explained.

"But you know I'm going out with

Mitch tonight!"

"I can fix it." Zoe wielded the silver pair of scissors.

"No." Lauren looked down at the floor, where half inch strands of light brown hair had fallen – apart from a piece that looked more like one inch. "I think this was a bad idea."

"But you said your hair was getting too long, nearly touching your shoulders," Zoe countered. "I thought this would be the perfect solution. Just a little trim before your date tonight."

"I'll have to wear my hair in a bun or a ponytail." Lauren pulled her hair back and started twisting it into a knot. "If it's long enough!" She looked at her cousin in panic.

"You could wear it short like me," Zoe said heartily.

"Your style looks great on you," Lauren spoke the truth, "but I don't know if such a short cut would suit me. Besides, I'm used to wearing my hair like this, and I think Mitch likes it." Heat warmed her cheeks as she mentioned her detective boyfriend.

"What do you think, Annie?" Zoe

turned to the cat. "Should I even up Lauren's hair?"

Annie's green eyes widened as she stared at the scissors in Zoe's hand.

"Brrt." *No.*

"Huh." Zoe sounded disappointed. "Well, there is a new hair stylist in town – I walked past the salon yesterday during my lunchbreak, but I don't know if she's open right now."

"Let's find out!" Lauren jumped up from the kitchen chair they'd dragged into the bathroom.

"I'm sure I could fix your hair," Zoe muttered, as she followed Lauren and Annie.

The trio ran the Norwegian Forest Cat Café in Gold Leaf Valley, a small town in Northern California. Annie showed the customers to the table she chose for them, while Lauren made the cupcakes, and Zoe made lattes and cappuccinos alongside her cousin.

It had been a slow Thursday in January. It seemed most of their customers had decided to stay home on a cold day like today, so they'd decided to close thirty minutes early. Zoe had volunteered to give Lauren a little trim before her date tonight, and Lauren had warily accepted. Now she wished she hadn't.

"Where's the salon?" Lauren grabbed her car keys from the kitchen table.

"Where the old salon was," Zoe replied, slinging a small black purse over her shoulder. "Sandra retired last month, and now someone else seems to have bought it."

"Oh, that's right." Lauren's brow cleared. "I'd heard that Sandra was going to live with her daughter in Arizona."

"I hope she likes the heat in summer." Zoe scrunched her nose.

"Brrt?" Annie asked as she watched them head toward the back door.

"We won't be long," Lauren told her. "I'm going to get my hair fixed." She fingered a roughly chopped strand.

"Brrt!" Annie sounded approving.

"Everyone's a critic," Zoe grumbled as she followed her cousin out the door.

Lauren jumped into her white compact car and started the engine.

"I don't want to waste time walking there in case she closes soon," she

4

explained as she drove down the street.

"I really thought I could cut your hair," Zoe told her earnestly.

"I know." Lauren smiled briefly at her.

Zoe had a good heart and a positive attitude that could be infectious. She was also impulsive at times, but Lauren knew her actions came from a good place.

"She's open!" Lauren snagged a parking spot right outside the small salon. The street was nearly deserted in the waning daylight, but the lights were on in the shop.

Lauren rushed inside, not even waiting for Zoe to join her.

She caught her breath in the reception area. A few comfortable looking chairs and a rack of magazines decorated the waiting area. Four stations with large mirrors, and a shampoo station made up the rest of the space.

"Hi." A slim girl maybe a couple of years older than Lauren's twenty-six left a customer with a plastic cap on her hair and came to the counter. "May I help you?"

"Can you fix this?" Lauren held out the offending shorter strands at the back of her head and turned around so the stylist could see.

"No problem." The stylist smiled at her, looking neat and efficient in denim jeans and a black sweater. Her chestnut locks had attractive reddish highlights, cut in a long bob with feathered ends. The hair color flattered her friendly green eyes.

"Now?" Lauren asked hopefully.

"I cut it." Zoe appeared by her side.

"It's easy to fix," the stylist told them. "I'm Brooke, by the way."

Lauren and Zoe introduced themselves.

"I can neaten you up right away." She gestured to Lauren to follow her to a station in front of a large mirror.

Lauren sank down on the black padded chair while Brooke wrapped a white cape around her.

A large hooded hair dryer hummed in the background, a woman sitting underneath it flicking through a magazine. She glanced up, then locked her gaze on the page once more.

"Thank you," Lauren said in relief as Brooke fetched the scissors.

"It will only take a few minutes," she told Lauren. "Unless you'd like me to give you some layers?"

"Umm ... no," Lauren replied. "Not right now, I don't think." She'd worn her light brown hair just below her chin for a while now, and thought Mitch liked it this way. So did she.

"I love your subtle golden highlights," Brooke said as she started snipping.

"Thanks," Lauren replied. "They're natural. I love your hair color, though."

"The chestnut is real but I go to an amazing colorist in Sacramento," Brooke replied. "I like coloring hair but she takes it to a whole new level. Let me know if you ever need her details."

"Thanks." Lauren smiled at Brooke in the mirror. "But isn't recommending someone else bad for your business?"

"Probably." Brooke nodded. "This is my first salon. I only opened yesterday. But I think honesty is best, especially in this profession."

"I think the same."

"Zoe's haircut is really cute," Brooke said, snipping away at the back of Lauren's hair. "I like pixie cuts. Did

Sandra do it?"

"No," Lauren replied. "We usually get our hair cut in Sacramento on our day off."

"What do you do?" Brooke looked interested.

Lauren told her about the café.

"Oh, I must visit," Brooke said. "I love cats."

"Are you a local?" Lauren asked.

"No, but I hope to be." Brooke smiled at Lauren's reflection. "I grew up in Sacramento. But when I found out that the owner was retiring and this place was for sale, I jumped at the chance."

"There were always women getting their hair done here whenever I walked past," Lauren told her.

"That's good to know. I looked through the books but it's nice to get an unbiased opinion."

Brooke finished trimming Lauren's hair, then gave it a quick blow dry.

"There," she said with satisfaction as she handed Lauren a mirror so she could check the back. "What do you think?"

"Thank you." Lauren smiled with relief. Her hair looked exactly the same before Zoe had touched it, although a little shorter.

"You're welcome." Brooke whisked off the cape and walked her to the register.

"It looks good." Zoe put down a fashion magazine. "Thank you." Relief flitted across her face.

The door opened and a bouquet of flowers appeared – sunny yellow gerberas jostled for space among golden roses, with paperwhites and pink tulips rounding out the selection.

"Order for Brooke." A man's voice sounded from behind the blooms.

"That's me," Brooke said, rounding the counter.

The man lowered the bouquet. "I need you to sign here." He held out a clipboard.

He appeared to be in his early thirties. His shaggy sandy hair seemed to be in need of a cut, and he wore a gray coat, with a cream button-down shirt tucked neatly into brown slacks. His blue eyes were framed with square navy metal glasses.

Brooke scratched her signature with

the chunky purple pen he gave to her. She blushed as her finger brushed his.

"I hope you like them." He smiled shyly at her. "I'm Jeff, by the way. I run the flower shop in town."

She scanned the card. "They're from my parents – to congratulate me on opening the salon."

"They were supposed to arrive yesterday. I'm sorry." Jeff sounded rueful. "There was a hold up in the deliveries and I didn't have enough flowers to make up the bouquet until today."

"It doesn't matter," she assured him, closing her eyes and inhaling the sweet scents from the blooms. "They're beautiful."

"Thank you," he answered

Lauren and Zoe watched the exchange. Lauren held her wallet, ready to pay the stylist.

"Look at my hair!" A human cyclone stormed into the salon. "Look!" She pointed to her mahogany hair. Limp curls drooped unevenly from the top of her head, brushing the tops of her shoulders.

Brooke bit her lip as she stared at the

newcomer. "Did you wash your hair yesterday?" she asked.

"Of course I did." The woman, who looked to be in her mid-thirties, replied. Her forehead wrinkled in annoyance. "I *could not* stand the smell of the solution a minute longer. As soon as I got home I gave my hair a good shampoo."

"I told you not to do that," Brooke said quietly. "Otherwise you could get this result."

"I want my money back!" The woman scowled at Brooke. She looked ugly in the moment. "Do you hear me?"

"Everyone can hear you, Paula," the woman with the plastic cap on her head called out. She waved to her friend, the movement highlighting a bracelet with a turquoise bead.

"Helen, is that you?" Paula narrowed her eyes.

"Yes." The plastic capped woman nodded. "I took your advice and decided to visit the salon."

The woman under the big hair dryer had put down the magazine and watched the scene unfold.

"That was before my hair was ruined!"

Paula noticed the woman under the hair dryer. "What are you looking at, Rhonda?"

The woman flushed and reached for her magazine.

Paula glanced at Lauren and Zoe, then did a doubletake as she noticed Jeff, the flower delivery guy.

"What are you doing here?" she demanded.

Jeff shifted, then squared his shoulders. "Doing my job. Delivering flowers."

"Huh." She sounded dismissive, and turned her attention back to Brooke. "What are you going to do about my hair?"

"I can fix it for you," Brooke replied, "but I won't be able to re-perm it for at least two weeks. Your hair has undergone a major chemical process and needs a chance to recover."

"Two weeks!" Paula looked aghast. "I can't walk around town for two weeks looking like this!" She pointed at her limp curls. "I need it re-permed *now*!"

"I don't think that's a good idea," Brooke told her. "Why don't I make an appointment for you in two weeks' time and then we can discuss your options?"

"You could wear a hat," Helen called out. "It *is* winter."

Paula looked unimpressed as she watched the stylist turn the pages of a large appointment book. "Aren't you computerized?"

"It's quicker and easier to use this." Brooke tapped an open page. "And if I have computer problems, I'll still have access to all my appointments. What about Tuesday afternoon in two weeks?"

"I suppose," Paula said grudgingly, giving the stylist a death stare. "But I expect you to cover the cost. I'm not shelling out more money for something that hasn't worked."

Lauren watched Brooke's mouth open, as if she were about to say something, then shut. When the stylist spoke, it was in a pleasant tone.

"All right. I'll see you then." She handed a card to the woman, who stormed out of there, not even acknowledging her friend.

"I'm sorry about Paula," Jeff said awkwardly. "She has a tendency to blow

13

up and hates being in the wrong."

"How do you know?" Zoe asked, then seemed to realize what she'd said. "Sorry. It's none of my business."

"We were married," he replied. "But we're divorced now."

Lauren paid Brooke, thanking her once again for her expertise.

Jeff left just before they did. Lauren notice Brooke's gaze linger on him for a second as he departed.

"Well, that was interesting." Zoe shuddered as they left the salon. "I hope that woman never visits the café."

"I hope not, too," Lauren replied. She knew a lot of the locals by sight, if not by name, but she hadn't met Paula before, or Jeff the flower guy.

"Hey, did you notice that Paula's friend was wearing one of the bracelets I made? But I sold it to a man."

"Maybe that was her husband?" Lauren suggested.

Zoe had set up a little display in the café a few weeks ago with a couple of her two-toned bracelets. Only one of them had sold, though.

"That could be it." Zoe nodded. "At

least, I think it was my bracelet."

CHAPTER 2

The next morning, Lauren crunched granola at the kitchen table, while Zoe munched on whole wheat toast.

"How did your date go with Mitch last night?" Zoe mumbled around a mouthful.

Lauren swallowed. "Good." She smiled.

"Did he notice your hair?"

"Uh-huh." Warmth flickered through her as she thought about last night. Mitch had noticed her slightly shorter hair right away, and had chuckled when she'd told him what had happened.

"What about Chris?" Lauren now asked her cousin.

"Brrt?" Annie sounded enquiring, too. She'd finished her breakfast but now kept them company at the table.

Zoe wrinkled her nose.

"We don't have anything planned right now," she finally said.

Chris was Mitch's friend. Last year, Zoe had delved into the world of internet dating, only to be disappointed. The last fiasco had involved Chris's younger brother. When Chris found out about it,

16

he had apologized profusely for his brother's actions, and Zoe had warily accepted his apology. They had gone on a couple of dates since then, but Lauren wasn't sure how Zoe felt about him.

"He's working as a paramedic in Sacramento," Zoe added, as she spread butter on another piece of toast. "And then it takes him an hour to drive down here, or for me to drive up there."

"Maybe we could double date one night," Lauren suggested, wanting to cheer her up. Zoe had mentioned that possibility a couple of months ago.

"Maybe," Zoe said thoughtfully. "Yep, that might be a good idea."

They finished their breakfast and then trooped down the private hallway to the café. Lauren had inherited her grandmother's coffee shop, with the attached Victorian cottage. The only thing she had changed was to turn the regular café into a certified cat café, with Annie the only feline in residence.

"Beading club tonight," Zoe said cheerfully as she unstacked the chairs from the pine tables.

"Don't you mean

knitting/crochet/string-art/beading?"
Lauren teased, listing all the hobbies Zoe
had tried since quitting online dating.

"Brrt!" Annie seemed to agree as she
hopped up on her pink cat bed on a low
wall shelf, preparing to "supervise".

"I think I'll make a necklace next,"
Zoe mused as the chair she handled
scraped on the wooden floorboards. "I've
already made earrings and a bracelet for
myself."

"And a bangle for me, and one for
Mrs. Finch," Lauren added. She loved the
bead jewelry her cousin had designed for
her and wished she could wear it at work,
but worried that it would get in the way
of making lattes and baking cupcakes.

"I'd better bake the first batch of
cupcakes." She hurried into the kitchen.

Lauren usually whipped up the cake
batter the day before, and yesterday had
been no exception.

She spooned vanilla, and cinnamon
swirl batter into the tins and slid them
into the pre-heated oven.

Soon, their pastry chef, Ed, would
arrive. His featherlight Danish was
legendary in the small town.

Lauren and Zoe bustled around the empty café, getting it ready for their first customers. Lauren hoped today would be busier than yesterday. She looked out of the large window in the seating area – although cold, the sky was a clear blue. She just hoped her regular customers wouldn't let the chilly temperature discourage them.

The banging of tins from the kitchen sounded Ed's arrival. Lauren knew better than to disturb him with small talk. He was more of the strong, silent type, with monster rolling pins for arms and wild short auburn hair.

"Ooh, Ed's here," Zoe remarked. She zoomed to the swinging kitchen doors. "I want to find out how AJ is."

"Brrt!" Annie jumped down from her bed and joined Zoe. Although it was a cat café, the Norwegian Forest Cat wasn't allowed in the commercial kitchen.

"Let me know," Lauren replied. Annie had found the little brown tabby under a bush in the back garden. Ed immediately adopted the tiny scrap and was now a fond cat dad.

Zoe came out of the kitchen several

seconds later and smiled down at Annie.

"She's fine, and Ed says I can arrange a play date with her and Annie."

"Brrt!" *Good!*

"AJ must be around five months now," Lauren mused as she unlocked the entrance door.

"Yep." Zoe nodded, her pixie bangs brushing her forehead. "And Ed said she's eating well and putting on weight."

"That's good to hear." The tiny kitten had seemed undernourished when Annie had found her, and Lauren wondered if AJ had been the runt of the litter.

"Brrp." Annie looked pleased at the news.

"When would you like to get together with AJ?" Zoe bent down to the silver-gray tabby. "Today? Tomorrow?"

"Ed doesn't work Saturdays," Lauren reminded her. The café was open from nine-thirty to five Tuesdays to Fridays, and open until lunchtime on Saturdays.

"Pooh. That's right." Zoe tapped her cheek. "And it's club night tonight. I could always go and pick up AJ and bring her here to play with Annie."

"That sounds like an idea." Lauren

glanced at Annie, whose ears had pricked up at the suggestion. "What about tomorrow afternoon? If it's okay with Ed," she added hastily.

"I'll find out!" Zoe zipped back to the kitchen, the swinging doors barely closing before she rushed out again. "Ed says okay!"

"Brrt!"

The entrance door opened and two women appeared in the doorway.

Lauren exchanged a glance with Zoe – they'd seen the newcomers yesterday, at the salon!

"Brrt?" Annie trotted up to the pair, who hovered at the *Please Wait to be Seated* sign.

"Annie will show you to a table," Lauren told them.

"Really?" The woman with the perm disaster frowned as she glanced at her friend. Today, she wore her droopy waves in a tight knot, most of her head covered with a blue messy bun beanie.

Lauren recognized her friend as the woman getting the deep conditioning treatment.

But instead of a plastic cap around her

hair, this morning she wore her ash brown locks in a wavy bob. Her fuzzy green sweater and gray slacks seemed a comfortable fit on her plump frame.

"I've heard about this cat," the friend replied, looking down at Annie. "You *are* a pretty cat."

"Brrp," Annie said, as if agreeing.

She swiveled on her paws and sauntered to a two-seater table in the middle of the room.

"Brrt." *You sit here.*

The two women looked at each other, the woman with the perm shrugging before sinking onto the wooden chair.

There was a menu on each table, requesting that customers order at the counter. Lauren and Zoe relaxed this rule for the elderly, infirm, or otherwise harried person.

After a few minutes, neither customer came to the counter, Lauren and Zoe looked at each other. Annie was now resting in her cat bed.

"I'll go," Lauren told her cousin.

"What can I get you?" She approached the table, whipping out her little notepad and pencil from the pocket of her apron.

She and Zoe wore a casual uniform to work, on Lauren's part consisting of capris and t-shirt in the warmer months, and jeans cut for her curvy figure and a sweater in the colder months.

"I'm dying for a coffee," the deep conditioning woman said. "I've cut out caffeine for eight months but I miss it *so much*."

"I told you it was no good for you, Helen," Paula informed her. "I really don't think you should start back on it."

"I'm sure just one latte won't hurt," her friend replied. She looked hopefully at Lauren. "Will it?"

"I hope not," Lauren replied, thinking of the two mochas and one cappuccino she'd enjoyed the day before.

"Actually," Zoe jumped into the conversation, joining them at the table, "I read an article a few weeks ago saying it was okay to have up to six single espressos per day."

"Really?" Helen looked excited. *"Six?"*

"Yep," Zoe replied. "Six. And Lauren and I don't drink that many per day, and we're fine."

"I don't think you should believe everything you read," Paula muttered. "Because the article I read last year said coffee was bad for you. That's why I told Helen here to stop drinking it."

Lauren surveyed the two women. Paula with the perm seemed a few years younger than her friend, yet had a slightly bossy attitude toward her.

"One latte won't kill me," Helen replied. "And I'd love to have a cupcake too. What sort do you have?"

"Vanilla, and cinnamon swirl today," Lauren replied.

"They're awesome," Zoe enthused.

After a couple of minutes of discussion, the women decided.

Lauren took their order and hurried back to the counter, Zoe by her side.

"I can make the latte and green tea if you plate the cinnamon swirls."

"Roger, boss." Zoe grinned.

In a few minutes, Lauren carried the order to the table. On the surface of the regular latte was a peacock. She and Zoe had attended an advanced latte art class last year, and were now able to produce swans and peacocks, as well as the usual hearts, tulips, and rosettas.

"I can't believe how badly my perm turned out," Paula grumbled to her friend.

"That's because you washed it when the stylist told you not to." Helen glanced appreciatively at the cupcake Lauren gave her, a large swirl of frosting with a sprinkle of golden Ceylon cinnamon on top.

Paula scowled. "Maybe she shouldn't have used such a stinky perm solution. That's the only reason I washed it straight away."

Helen pursed her lips but didn't say anything.

"I don't know if I'll keep my appointment with her in two weeks," Paula continued. "I'm not sure that I can trust her to do a proper job." She shrugged. "I'm seriously thinking of going somewhere in Sacramento where they know what they're doing, and leaving a bad review for the place here."

"Don't do that!" Helen looked horrified. "Brooke seems like a nice person and didn't do anything wrong. *You* did."

Paula rolled her eyes and glanced at

Lauren, as if seeing her properly for the first time. "Weren't you at the salon yesterday?" she demanded.

"I'd just gotten my hair cut," Lauren replied.

"I'm glad I went there," Helen said. "Look at my hair – that deep conditioning treatment really did the trick." Her ash brown hair looked glossy and well nourished.

"Hmph." Paula sniffed, looking unimpressed.

Her friend raised her eyebrows, but didn't say anything.

Lauren made her way back to the counter.

"What did they say?" Zoe hissed in her ear.

"Paula is thinking of leaving a bad review for Brooke's salon," Lauren told her the short version.

"No way!" Zoe's mouth parted in an O.

A few more customers came in, taking up their attention. Once they'd received their orders, Lauren noticed Paula waving in her direction. Lauren hurried over to the table.

"Would you like something else?" she asked politely. Both plates were empty, and it looked like they'd finished their beverages as well.

"Where do we pay?" Paula demanded, pulling out her gray leather wallet from her matching handbag.

"Over at the counter." Lauren gestured to where Zoe stood.

"Thank you," Helen murmured.

A minute later, the two women arrived at the cash register.

"I do miss my quilting," Helen was saying to her friend as they pulled out cash from their wallets.

"But you said it was making you miserable," her friend countered, giving Lauren the correct money.

"Not exactly," Helen murmured, as she handed over her share, including a tip. "I said it was costing me more money than I thought to create designs, and you said I should take a break from it for a while. And I have."

"So what's the problem?" Paula asked as she moved toward the door.

"I want to start doing it again." Helen smiled at Lauren and Zoe before following her friend.

"Do you really think that's a good idea?" Paula queried. "I thought your husband didn't like you spending so much money on it."

"He said last night we could rejig our budget so I could afford to buy some new fabric." Helen sounded excited at the thought.

"Have you really thought about this?" Paula's voice floated from the entrance as they exited the café.

"Wow," Zoe murmured to Lauren. "She really doesn't want Helen to do quilting." She shuddered. "Not that *I* would want to." Zoe was not known for her sewing.

"Here's your tip." Lauren clinked the coins into the jar on the counter. Since she owned the café, she didn't think it right to participate in the tips. Zoe and Ed shared them. But as well as a salary for herself, Lauren paid Zoe and Ed a decent wage.

"Thanks." Zoe smiled, then her expression dropped a little. "The perm woman Paula didn't leave me – or Ed – anything. What a cheapskate."

"Maybe she couldn't afford to," Lauren offered. "She's just been to the salon."

"Yeah, maybe." But Zoe didn't sound convinced. Then she brightened. "Never mind. The tips are a nice little extra. I manage fine on what you pay me."

"Good." Lauren smiled.

"Hello, dears." The door opened and an elderly lady walked into the café, her cane tapping along the hardwood floors.

"Brrt!" Annie jumped down from her bed and ran to greet her.

"Hello, Annie, dear." Mrs. Finch bent down a tad.

"Hi, Mrs. Finch," Lauren greeted one of their favorite customers.

"Is that my bracelet?" Zoe's brown eyes sparkled as she spied the green and gold beads jangling on Mrs. Finch's wrist.

"Yes, it is." Mrs. Finch smiled, her rouged cheeks looking like orange California poppies. "It was so kind of you to make me one, Zoe. I wear it all the time."

"My pleasure," Zoe replied. Lauren knew she meant it.

"What can we get you today?" Lauren asked.

"One of your lovely lattes, please, and do you have any vanilla cupcakes?"

"Yes, we do," Zoe answered for her cousin.

"Brrt," Annie encouraged, ambling toward a table near the counter.

"I'm coming, Annie dear." Mrs. Finch slowly followed the feline.

Lauren made the coffee while Zoe plated the cupcake.

"I wonder if Mitch will stop by today," she said mischievously, glancing at Lauren.

"He said last night he wasn't sure if he'd have time," Lauren replied. "But we're having dinner tomorrow night."

"Anywhere nice?" Zoe teased.

"Sacramento," Lauren replied.

"Ooh, fancy." Zoe winked.

Lauren tried to tamp down the heat on her cheeks. She'd been dating Mitch since last year and had serious feelings for him. Although not much had been said in words, she'd gotten the impression he felt the same way.

Both of them took over Mrs. Finch's

order.

"I can't wait for tonight," Zoe told her as she set down the cupcake.

"Me, neither," Lauren said. "I think I've nearly finished knitting my hat and I'm looking forward to showing you."

"What about putting some beads in it?" Zoe's eyes sparkled. "We could start a new trend!"

"I'm sure we'll have fun tonight." Mrs. Finch picked up her cup with wobbly hands.

"Brrt!" Annie agreed, sitting on the chair opposite the senior. The four of them were the only members of the craft club.

To Lauren's relief, the rest of the day was a lot busier than yesterday. Mitch hadn't come in, though.

She looked at the clock with a start, registering it was a few minutes past five. The last customer had just departed.

"Time to lock up," Zoe said cheerfully, shooting the bolt home on the large oak door.

"Brrt!" Annie agreed, scampering to the private hallway.

"Do you want to go home first?"

Lauren unlocked the door and watched her run down the narrow passage and shimmy through the cat flap, entering the cottage kitchen. "See you soon."

"Brrp," came a distant reply.

"Maybe she wants to play with her toy hedgehog," Zoe suggested as she stacked chairs onto the tables.

"Sometimes I wish we didn't have to clean up at the end of the day." Lauren sighed as she plugged the vacuum into the wall socket. She and Zoe had done as much tidying up as they could that afternoon during the quieter periods.

"Let's have pizza for dinner." Zoe whipped out a phone from her jeans' pocket. "I'd suggest burgers, but we won't have much time for that."

"True." Lauren nodded. Gary's Burger Diner was a popular local eatery, but sadly didn't deliver.

Zoe phoned in the order, then they got the café ready for the morning.

"Awesome!" Zoe grinned as the delivery driver pulled up outside the café.

"Uh-huh." Lauren's stomach rumbled. Once they finished dinner, it would be practically time to go to Mrs. Finch's. In the warmer weather, they walked the block to her house, but now, in winter, and with twilight already surrounding the café, they'd planned to drive the short distance.

They ate their pizza in the cottage kitchen, Annie keeping them company. Lauren had already fed her one of her favorite meals, chicken in gravy.

"That was delish." Zoe licked her fingers after she finished her last piece, then wiped them on a napkin. "Now I'm good to go to Mrs. Finch's."

"Me too." Lauren rose and gathered the plates. "Why don't we do the dishes later?"

"Good idea." Zoe grinned.

Lauren placed the two plates in the sink and ran a little water in so they could soak.

"Annie, we're going to Mrs. Finch's now. Knitting club."

"Beading club," Zoe chimed in.

"Brrt!" *Annie club.*

They piled into Lauren's car and drove around the block in the chilly dark to Mrs. Finch's.

Their friend ushered them into her

sweet Victorian home.

Once they were settled in her living room decorated in tones of fawn and beige, Mrs. Finch said, "Do catch me up with what you've been doing this week, girls."

Although she usually came into the café every day, sometimes there wasn't enough time to fill her in on everything, especially if they were busy with customers. However, Annie usually sat with Mrs. Finch for the entirety of her visit.

Lauren and Zoe told her about the new hair salon, while Lauren knitted her red hat, and Zoe threaded beads onto another bracelet, this time using shades of orange and yellow.

Annie interjected with the occasional "Brrt!" dividing her time between the three of them.

"I'd heard Sandra had retired and was selling her salon," Mrs. Finch said. "Someone at the senior center said she was selling some of her hair dryers as well. She'd ordered too many, apparently, before she decided to retire. She always did my hair, but I'm afraid it's a bit of an effort for me sometimes to get out and about, so I haven't been for a while."

Lauren looked closely at Mrs. Finch's gray hair, caught up in a bun on top of her head. It did look a little untidy.

"We can take you." Lauren and Zoe spoke at once.

"That is so kind of you, dears." Mrs. Finch beamed. "But I know you're both busy at the café. It's a shame the new stylist doesn't do home visits – that would be ideal."

Lauren, Zoe, and Annie looked at each other.

"We could ask her," Lauren said.

"Yeah!" Zoe patted her short hair. "After Lauren's haircut, I was thinking of getting a little trim. And she *is* a lot closer than Sacramento."

"You could go on Monday – our day off," Lauren said.

"While I'm there I'll ask Brooke about home visits," Zoe finished.

"That would be wonderful." Mrs. Finch smiled. "You girls are so good to me – all of you."

"You're our friend," Lauren told her.

"Brrt!"

They made coffee using Mrs. Finch's pod machine, then carried on with their crafting. Zoe tried to convince Lauren to add some gold beads to her hat, but Lauren wasn't sure she wanted a bit of bling. She was pleased with the way her hat was coming along – it would match the scarf she'd finally finished knitting last year – and was now thinking of making Mitch a hat to go with the fawn scarf she'd knitted him for Christmas.

After a pleasant evening, they said goodbye to Mrs. Finch and drove home.

"I can't wait for Annie and AJ's play date tomorrow," Zoe said as they entered the cottage kitchen.

"Brrt!" *Me too!*

"I think Annie agrees with you." Lauren smiled as she looked fondly at the cat.

"Brrt!"

***

The next morning, Lauren looked forward to closing the café at lunchtime and spending time with Annie and AJ.

She wasn't sure how long Zoe planned on making the play date last, but she'd need some time to get ready for her date with Mitch tonight. He hadn't told her where they were going for dinner in Sacramento, only that he wanted it to be a surprise.

"Let's go!" Zoe put her coffee cup down on the kitchen table. "If it's not too busy today, maybe we can close a few minutes early."

"Like we did on Thursday?" Lauren teased.

"Brrt!" Annie agreed.

"Okay." Lauren said. "You're not the only ones who look forward to having a break on Saturday afternoons."

The trio trooped to the café through the private hallway. Annie sniffed the corners of the café, and apparently not finding anything interesting from the clean floor, sat in her cat bed, keeping an eye on proceedings.

Lauren and Zoe unstacked the chairs and got everything ready for their first customers, including fresh batches of vanilla, and triple chocolate ganache cupcakes.

"Time to open up." Zoe scooted to the entrance door and pulled back the bolt.

"No customers," she said a second later after sticking her head out into the street.

"You seem very eager this morning," Lauren said as she poured coffee beans into the hopper.

"I guess I'm just looking forward to this afternoon." Zoe grinned. "Oh, and Chris texted me last night," she added a little casually.

"He did? When?" Lauren crinkled her brow.

"I checked my phone when we got home from Mrs. Finch's," Zoe admitted. "And he'd sent it earlier last evening."

"What did he say?" Lauren asked. "It's okay if you don't want to tell me," she said hastily. "I'm not trying to be nosy."

"I know you're not," Zoe assured her. "He suggested we see a movie."

"Are you going to?" Lauren hoped her cousin's fledgling romance with Chris would work out. He seemed a nice guy, and a good match for Zoe.

"Maybe," Zoe replied. She stifled a grin. "Yes, okay, I will."

"Good."

"Brrt!" Annie added from her cat bed.

The door swung open and a girl with chestnut hair walked in.

"Brooke!" Lauren waved to her from the counter.

"Brrp?" Annie jumped down from the bed and ran to the *Please Wait to be Seated* sign.

"Is this your cat?" Brooke smiled as she bent down to greet the feline.

"This is Annie," Lauren told her.

"She'll choose a table for you," Zoe added.

"Really?"

"That's right," Lauren told her.

"Brrt." Annie led the way to a small table near the counter.

The hair stylist slowly followed, glancing around the café as she did so.

"I love your place," she told them as she sat down. Her table was close enough to the counter that she didn't have to shout. Annie hopped up on the empty chair and studied her.

"Thanks." Lauren surveyed the décor, seeing it with fresh eyes. The interior walls were pale yellow, complementing the pine tables and chairs. A string-art picture of a cupcake with lots of pink frosting decorated one of the walls – evidence of one of Zoe's previous hobbies.

"What can we get you?" Zoe zipped over.

"What do you recommend?" Brooke picked up the menu and scanned it.

"Lauren's cupcakes, for sure," Zoe enthused. "And you must try a mocha."

"Definitely." Brooke smiled.

"Ooh, do you do hair home visits?" Zoe said.

"No – well, I haven't really thought about it," Brooke told her.

"We don't mean to bombard you." Lauren came around the counter. "But we have a friend who'd like to get her hair done, but—"

"It's difficult for her to come to the salon," Zoe finished.

"What would she like done?" Brooke asked.

"I think a trim," Lauren began, "but—"

"We didn't think to ask exactly what Mrs. Finch wanted," Zoe chimed in.

"Oh, Sandra, the lady who sold the

salon to me, mentioned her regulars, including a Mrs. Finch," Brooke told them.

"It must be the same Mrs. Finch," Zoe assured her. "She's the only one we know, isn't she, Lauren?"

"That's right." Lauren nodded.

"Let me see what I can do," Brooke said. "I'm still getting established and I don't want to turn away any customers, but I'll need to find time to visit her – I could probably see her in the evening. Do you think that would work?"

Lauren and Zoe told her they'd check with Mrs. Finch and get back to her.

"Maybe we should just give them each other's phone numbers and they can set it up themselves," Zoe whispered as she made Brooke a large mocha.

"I think we should check with Mrs. Finch first," Lauren murmured as she plated a triple chocolate ganache cupcake.

"I guess," Zoe replied as she wiggled the milk jug so a peacock appeared on the surface of the micro foam. "Look!" she pointed at the bird. "I've been practicing."

"It looks awesome." Lauren admired the design.

Zoe carried the creation over to Brooke, who seemed impressed. Lauren followed with the sweet treat.

Annie still perched on the opposite chair, seeming to keep the hair stylist company.

They chatted with Brooke for a few minutes, then several customers trickled in.

"Forget what I said about closing early today," Zoe murmured two hours later. The trickle had turned into a flood.

"Maybe they're making up for not coming in on Thursday," Lauren replied. There had been no rain this morning, just a chilly cold temperature, which had seemed to encourage the locals to order cappuccinos, lattes, and mochas.

"Hi, gals!" Their curly gray-haired friend Martha barreled in, pushing her rolling walker. "Can't wait to have one of your hot chocolates, Zoe. With plenty of marshmallows."

"Coming right up." Zoe grinned. They'd met Martha last year when they'd joined together to save the senior center from being demolished by a developer.

"Brrp." Annie jumped down from her seat at Brooke's table, and ran to the senior. "Brrp?" She patted the vinyl seat of the walker with her paw.

"Hop on, cutie pie." Martha beamed.

Annie leaped onto the walker and allowed Martha to push the contraption. She usually asked Martha for a ride every time she visited the café, and now the rolling motion was familiar to her. Her green eyes were wide and sparkling, her paws pressing securely on the padded seat as they wheeled through the café.

"Brrt," she said to Martha as they approached an empty table.

"This one?" Martha asked, stopping.

"Brrp." *Yes.*

Annie scampered down from the walker and settled into one of the chairs.

"It's good to sit down sometimes." Martha sank down onto the pine chair.

"Would you like something to eat with your hot chocolate?" Lauren asked as she approached the table. She'd left Zoe busy making lattes. Although Martha was capable of pushing the walker to the counter, she looked like she needed a rest.

"Don't tempt me," Martha replied. "One of your vanilla cupcakes would be good."

"Of course." Lauren scratched a note on her pad.

"You look busy today," Martha observed.

Most of the tables were filled now and the low buzz of chatter and laughter permeated the air, along with the aroma of cherry and spice from the freshly ground coffee beans.

"It's good to see," Lauren admitted. She'd been a little worried on Thursday with the lack of customers, but hadn't liked to say anything to Zoe. This morning more than made up for that day, though.

"Everyone's still talking about this place at the senior center," Martha said.

"We appreciate the business," Lauren told her. She recognized some faces from the senior center party they'd catered last year.

"Whenever someone asks Denise where to get the best coffee, she always recommends you." Martha winked.

"That's nice of her." Lauren smiled at the thought of the new director of the center doing that.

She hurried to the counter to get Martha's order.

"Here's the hot chocolate." Zoe placed a large mug crammed with pink and white marshmallows on a tray.

"And here's the cupcake." Lauren used tongs to plate the vanilla frosted treat. "I'll take it over." She checked the tickets. "You're slammed."

"Thanks." Zoe pressed the button on the grinder, a low growl filling the air as coffee poured into the portafilter.

Usually Lauren made the coffees with Zoe as her back up, but today her cousin was the point girl.

At lunchtime, the last of the crowd dispersed, as if they suddenly remembered the café would be closing. Lauren disliked reminding people and sometimes stayed open a little longer so a customer could finish their coffee.

"Phew!" Zoe sank onto a chair after locking the door. "I certainly didn't expect it to be so busy."

"Nor did I," Lauren admitted. She

couldn't wait to go home next door and put her feet up. Except she couldn't.

"Now we have Annie and AJ's play date."

"Brrt!" Annie's green eyes sparkled. She'd joined them at the table closest to the counter.

"We just have to clean up first," Lauren told her.

"Brrp." Annie's lower lip jutted out for a second.

"We won't be long," Zoe promised her.

Lauren and Zoe stacked the chairs on the table. Zoe zoomed around with the vacuum while Lauren tackled the dirty dishes in the commercial kitchen.

For a second she wondered at the fact that Mitch hadn't stopped by, then told herself not to be silly. She was seeing him tonight, and they'd had dinner Thursday night.

"I grabbed paninis for our lunch." Zoe appeared in the kitchen, waving a paper bag.

"Good thinking." Lauren pulled off her rubber gloves. "The dishes are done. And I'm starving." They'd ended up being so busy that she and Zoe hadn't had a chance for a break.

Annie led the way down the private hallway to the cottage.

"Chicken in gravy?" Lauren offered as soon as they entered the homey kitchen.

"Brrt," Annie agreed, sitting by her lilac bowl.

Lauren fed her, then sat down at the table. Zoe had already plated their lunch – turkey, lettuce, and cranberry paninis.

"Thanks," she said gratefully as she took her first bite.

The only sounds in the kitchen were munching (Lauren and Zoe) and lapping (Annie) as the three of them ate their lunch.

After they finished eating, Zoe grabbed Lauren's car keys.

"And now it's play date time!"

"Brrt!" Annie encouraged.

"I'll pick up AJ and bring her back here."

"Do you need to use Annie's carrier?" Lauren asked. "Or does Ed have one now?"

Zoe wrinkled her nose. "I hadn't thought that far ahead," she admitted.

"I'll take Annie's, just in case."

Lauren and Annie watched her hurry out of the cottage, the plastic cage banging against her legs.

"She won't be long," Lauren told Annie. "You and AJ will have a good time this afternoon."

"Brrt."

Lauren tidied up the kitchen, Annie 'supervising'. Before long, she heard a car pull up nearby, and her cousin's footsteps outside the back door.

"Here we are." Zoe entered the kitchen, carrying the cage. Inside was a Maine Coon brown tabby. Her fur was fawn with dark brown stripes. In the middle of her forehead was more dark brown fur in the shape of an M.

"Brrt!" Annie jumped down from the kitchen chair and ran to greet her friend.

"Mew!" AJ pawed the plastic bars of the carrier. "Mew!"

Zoe shut the door behind her and bent down to open the carrier.

"There you go, AJ." She grinned as the half-grown cat jumped out of the carrier.

"Brrt." Annie seemed to communicate silently with the tabby for a few seconds, then ran into the living room, AJ close behind.

"I wonder what they'll play with first." Zoe joined them in the living room.

Lauren followed, sitting down on the sofa while the cats chased a jingly ball around the room.

"I wish I was a cat." Zoe laughed as the two tabbies had fun with their game.

"Me too," Lauren admitted. She'd often wondered what it would be like to be Annie instead of having to do the accounts as well as running the café, and wondering why Mitch hadn't stopped to see her since their last date.

After chasing the ball, Annie and AJ investigated every room of the house. Annie led the way, AJ right behind her.

When they appeared in the living room again, Annie shared her furry toy hedgehog.

"Oh, look," Lauren whispered as the two cats curled up next to each other on the carpet, the brown stuffed creature between them. Each cat had a paw on the toy.

"I think they're snoozing." Zoe stifled a yawn. "I wish I could do that right now."

"I know what you mean," Lauren said ruefully. She just hoped she didn't fall asleep on Mitch tonight.

While the cats were sleeping, Lauren took the opportunity to catch up with her chick-lit novel. Zoe threaded beads onto her latest bracelet.

After a while, Zoe checked her watch. "I guess I'd better take AJ home to Ed." She didn't look like she wanted to. "I told him she'd be back there by four-thirty."

"Is it that time already?" Lauren's eyes widened as she glanced at her watch. Not yet. Phew.

Their low conversation seemed to rouse Annie.

"Brrp?" she asked sleepily.

"It's time for AJ to go home," Lauren told her.

"Brrp." Annie looked disappointed.

"I know how you feel," Lauren told her. "But Ed is expecting her to come home today."

"Mew?" It seemed the mention of Ed's name woke up AJ. She sat up, her brown eyes opening wide.

"Time to go home, sweetie," Zoe told

her regretfully.

The kitten stood up and nuzzled Annie for a few seconds.

"Mew," she told her.

"Brrt," Annie replied. She followed her friend to the carrier.

"I swear they understand every single word," Zoe marveled as she helped AJ into the cage.

"I really think they do." Lauren nodded. She waved goodbye to AJ as Zoe carried her to the car.

Annie let out a little sigh and wandered into the living room.

"I know," Lauren sympathized. "But it was fun having AJ here. I'm sure Ed will let her come over again."

"Brrt." Annie's expression lifted.

Lauren and Annie snuggled on the sofa, Annie 'reading' with her, her gaze focused on each page of the book.

"I'm home," Zoe called out before appearing in the doorway. She frowned at Lauren. "Shouldn't you be getting ready for your date?"

Lauren started. She'd enjoyed her quiet time with Annie so much, she'd forgotten to check her watch.

Five-thirty.

"It doesn't take an hour to drive to Ed's house and back," she said.

"I know." Zoe grinned. "I told Ed what a good time the two of them had, and he told me about a new recipe he was trying for honeyed walnut Danish. Then I got gas on the way home."

"You did?" It had been on Lauren's to-do list. "How much do I owe you?"

Zoe waved a hand in dismissal. "My treat. I've been using your car a lot lately."

"Thanks." Lauren smiled.

"Brrt?" Annie enquired.

"Want to help me get ready for my date with Mitch?" Lauren asked her.

"Brrt!" Annie ran down the hall toward Lauren's bedroom.

After a quick shower, Lauren decided on her new periwinkle wrap dress in a knit fabric and a black coat as it was chilly outside.

"What do you think, Annie?" Lauren asked once she was ready.

"Brrt!" Annie sat on the bed, her green eyes seeming to approve.

"That's what I think, too." Zoe peeked

52

in the doorway. "You'll knock him dead."

Lauren winced.

"Oops, bad choice of words." Zoe clapped a hand over her mouth.

More than one murder had taken place in the small town last year, and it wasn't something they liked to dwell on.

A ring sounded at the front door.

"He's here!" Zoe answered the door.

Lauren picked up her purse, hearing Zoe's muffled voice and Mitch's deeper tone.

"I'll see you later," she told Annie, giving her a gentle stroke.

Annie followed her to the front door.

"Hi," she said to Mitch.

"Hi." His warm brown eyes focused solely on her. He was tall, in his early thirties, with short dark hair and a straight nose. His lips curved up in a smile.

"Brrt?" Annie prompted after a minute.

"Right." He blinked. "Hi, Annie. "Ready to go, Lauren?"

"Yes." She turned to Zoe and Annie. "Have fun, you two."

"We will," Zoe assured her. "Won't we, Annie?"

"Brrt."

CHAPTER 3

Lauren sat opposite Mitch at a new to her upscale restaurant in Sacramento. Soft classical music played in the background. Tables with crisp white linen cloths and silver cutlery dotted the room.

She'd already filled him in on what had happened during the last two days, including Annie and AJ's play date.

Now, they were waiting for their entrees.

"I'm sorry I haven't stopped by the café lately," he told her. "I've been doing some overtime."

"Oh?"

"I was going to wait until dessert." He hesitated, then delved into his jacket pocket. "This is for you."

"What is it?" Her gaze was glued to the small black box. "You've already given me a Christmas present. The beautiful map of the stars." He'd also added his own message to it.

"This is something else. For being you." His gaze warmed her.

She carefully opened the box. Nestled

on a bed of satin was a gold chain necklace with the letter L.

"I didn't want to get you a bracelet because I thought it might get in the way when you're working in the café," he explained.

She was sure her cheeks were crimson – they certainly felt that way.

"Oh, Mitch, it's beautiful." Her finger traced the L. She lifted the piece of jewelry and held it against her neck.

"Let me fasten it for you." He pushed back his chair and came around to her. His fingers brushed the nape of her neck as he closed the clasp. "There."

"Thank you." She looked down at the L resting against her décolletage.

"I wanted to give you something special – because you're special to me," he said softly as he sat down again.

"You're special to me, too," she told him, blinking furiously. She was *not* going to cry.

The rest of the evening took on a dreamlike quality for Lauren – until the spell was rudely interrupted by a well-dressed portly man sneezing on her as they left the restaurant.

"Sorry," the stranger muttered, mopping his nose with a linen handkerchief before entering.

"I hope I don't catch a cold." Lauren furrowed her brow. Maybe that was why business had been so slow on Thursday – people had stayed home, feeling under the weather.

"Take a shower tonight," Mitch advised. "I'm sure you'll be okay."

Lauren nodded, determined not to let the incident ruin her evening. She glanced down at her necklace, the sight of the gold L instantly lifting her spirits.

As Mitch drove her home, they spoke about their plans for the following week, agreeing to go out Wednesday night.

"I hope Zoe and Annie aren't spying on us tonight," Lauren murmured when he pulled up outside her cottage.

"Let's risk it." He grinned.

He took her hand as they walked up the porch steps.

"I can't see anyone," Lauren said doubtfully, looking at the front window. On previous dates with Mitch, she'd learned later that the duo had peered out of the window to peek at them saying goodnight.

"Let's give them something to look at," Mitch suggested as he cupped Lauren's face.

"What if I'm infectious?" she countered.

"I'll risk it."

He kissed her tenderly, wiping the memory of being sneezed on out of her mind.

They said goodnight a few times, then Lauren finally let herself into the cottage.

"I'm home," she called out.

"We know." Zoe and Annie suddenly appeared in front of her, both of them smiling.

***

Zoe oohed and ahhed over Lauren's necklace, then nodded in understanding when Lauren said she was going to take a shower.

Lauren said goodnight to her cousin and went to bed, Annie nestled by her side. She put all thoughts of being sneezed on out of her mind, and thought about Mitch instead.

The next morning, all of them slept in – their Sunday treat unless they planned on going to church.

Lauren woke up, stretching, and swallowed. Oh, no. Her throat felt scratchy.

"I think I caught that man's cold." She looked at Annie with wide eyes.

"Brrt?"

"I think I'm getting a cold."

"Brrt!" Annie jumped off the bed and ran out of the bedroom.

"I don't think I'm infectious to you," she protested.

A couple of minutes later, Zoe appeared in the doorway, Annie by her side.

"What's wrong?" she asked. "Annie told me to come and check on you."

"I'm sorry I thought you were scared of catching my cold, Annie," Lauren apologized.

"Brrp." Annie hopped onto the bed and bunted Lauren's hand. All was forgiven.

Lauren told Zoe her suspicions.

"Oh, no! You haven't had a cold for ages. Neither have I."

"I know," Lauren agreed, her throat

suddenly feeling worse.

"Hot lemon and honey," Zoe declared. "And wrap up so you don't catch a chill. Ooh, and lots of tissues."

"I think we've got all those," Lauren replied.

"Good. You'd better rest today and tomorrow. Lucky the café is closed then."

Lauren nodded.

"If your throat hurts, try not to talk too much."

Lauren didn't think that would be a problem, since Zoe was the more talkative of the two of them.

She spent the rest of the day following Zoe's advice. If her throat wasn't sore, it would have been very pleasant to relax on the sofa and finish reading her book, Annie by her side. She just hoped she would be better by Tuesday. She didn't want to infect her customers, or Zoe.

Zoe was super solicitous, anticipating Lauren's needs.

"You'd make a great nurse," she told her cousin that afternoon.

"I can just see it. Nurse Zoe." She struck a pose. "I wonder what I'd look like in a nurse's uniform." She giggled.

Lauren went to bed early that night. Surely with all the warm water, and honey and lemon beverages she'd had that day she would be better by morning?

But it was not to be. Her throat was still scratchy when she woke up on Monday.

"Brtt?" *How are you feeling?*

"The same." Lauren wrinkled her nose.

"Brrt." Annie sounded disappointed.

"I know," she said softly, stroking Annie's velvet soft fur.

Lauren had a quick shower, hoping the warm water would work some magic. For breakfast, she made herself some oatmeal, but after a few spoonfuls, didn't feel like eating anymore.

"Oh, no." Zoe walked into the kitchen and peered at her. "You're still sick."

"Yep."

"Will you be okay while I get my hair cut this morning? If I go early enough I mightn't need an appointment."

"I'll come with you." Lauren took a gulp of orange juice. "Maybe the fresh air will do me some good."

"You think?" Zoe sounded skeptical.

Lauren gazed out of the kitchen

window. The sky was clear blue.

"I'll be fine." She tried to believe that.

"Well, okay," Zoe replied. "But if you start sneezing, you'd better come straight home."

"Yes, Mom," Lauren teased, her voice a little husky.

"Brrt?" Annie asked. She sat on the kitchen chair next to Lauren.

"I don't think Lauren should come with me to the hair salon, but she's insisting," Zoe told the cat. She put a piece of whole wheat bread into the toaster. "You'd better wrap up warm," she told Lauren.

"So had you," Lauren replied. "It's only a scratchy throat, Zoe. I'll be fine." She willed herself to believe it.

After breakfast, Lauren put on her coat plus the scarf she'd knitted for herself last year.

"It's a shame you haven't finished knitting your hat," her cousin said. "You could have worn that, too."

Zoe was wrapped up in her colorful crocheted scarf and a red puffer jacket.

"On the way home we could stop by Mrs. Finch's and arrange her home hair appointment with Brooke," Zoe suggested.

"Good idea," Lauren replied. "I won't stand too near Mrs. Finch though, just in case."

They said goodbye to Annie and stepped outside. Lauren thought a bracing walk to the salon would be beneficial.

By the time they got there, she'd had second thoughts. She should have stayed at home. Her throat felt worse and now she seemed to have developed a case of the sniffles.

"Zoe, I'm going back home because—"

"Wait." Zoe clutched her arm. "What's that?"

They'd just turned the corner and were facing the salon. The street was deserted at just after nine.

A heap of clothes lay on the sidewalk outside the salon. The lights were off and the shop seemed closed.

A cold feeling clutched Lauren's stomach, a contrast to her hot, irritated throat.

"Oh, no," she whispered. "Not another dead body."

CHAPTER 4

Zoe took a step toward the bundle, then shuffled backward.

"Maybe we should just call 911 now," she suggested.

"Without checking to see exactly what it is?" Lauren croaked.

"Okay." Zoe drew in a deep breath and strode right up to the heap. Lauren followed – and gasped at the sight.

Paula, the woman who had her hair permed last week and had washed it too soon, lay on the cold sidewalk, the cord of a hair dryer wrapped around her throat, strangling her.

Lauren's fingers fumbled for the phone in her purse. She dialed 911, then held out the device to her cousin. "You talk," she rasped.

She wasn't sure if it was stress, but her throat suddenly felt worse.

Zoe spoke rapidly into the phone, giving the address and their names.

"We have to wait here," she said glumly, shuddering as she turned away from the shopfront – and the body.

"Not again," Lauren muttered. "Do

you think we're jinxed?"

"I hope not." Zoe wrinkled her nose. "But maybe we'll discover who the killer is – just like last year."

Lauren nodded, wishing she could just go home and crawl into bed. It had definitely been a mistake to come out this morning. But if she hadn't – she shivered – Zoe would have been alone when she found Paula.

"I wonder where Brooke is?" Zoe frowned, peering at the salon windows from where she stood. "I thought she'd be open by now."

"Me, too." Lauren pointed to the times on the glass door. "It says she opens on Monday at nine."

"I hope the police get here soon." Zoe stamped her feet and tucked her hands into her coat pockets. She looked at Lauren sympathetically. "You really need to go home."

"Do I look that bad?" Lauren hoped Mitch wouldn't arrive on the scene.

"No." Zoe shook her head. "But you do look miserable."

"Thanks." Lauren grimaced.

A dark green car pulled up. Lauren

turned her head at the sound, at the same time noticing a speck of pink, like a tiny ball, near Paula's body. Before she had time to process it, Brooke greeted them.

"Hi guys," Brooke slammed the car door shut, and pulled her quilted blue jacket around her. "I'm sorry I'm late. Have you been waiting long?" She glanced at her watch.

"Don't come any closer." Zoe held up her hand in a stop motion.

"Why?" She took another couple of steps, then halted. "That's Paula!" she gasped. "And that's my hair dryer." She pointed with a trembling finger at the murder weapon. "And that's my salon." She focused on the shopfront, her gaze unwavering.

Brooke paled, her berry lip color standing out in stark contrast. "The police are going to think I did it!"

***

Lauren didn't know if it was a good thing or not that Mitch didn't show up. Instead, the scene was secured by uniformed officers, and after giving a brief statement, Lauren and Zoe were told they could go home.

"I hope Brooke is going to be okay," Zoe said as they hurried back to the cottage.

"Maybe they need to ask her more questions than us," Lauren managed, her throat feeling like it was on fire. "Because she owns the salon."

"That's probably it," Zoe agreed. "Although—" she tapped her cheek "—I wonder why she was late opening up this morning." She halted and stared at Lauren. "You don't think she killed Paula, do you?"

"I don't think anything right now," Lauren murmured. All she wanted to do was go home, sip a hot drink, and relax. Either on the sofa or in bed – she wasn't fussy.

Zoe peered at her face. "You definitely look worse now," she murmured.

"Thanks." Lauren grimaced.

"Come on, we'd better get home." Zoe took her arm. "I'll make you a honey and lemon drink. Then I'd better go to the store and stock up on OJ. I'm sure I read that fresh fruit juice can help a cold – all that vitamin C."

"Thanks." Lauren smiled wanly.

"I guess it is true that you can catch a cold if someone sneezes on you." Zoe shivered. "I hope nobody sneezes on *me*."

Lauren nodded, glad when the short walk was over and they stood in front of the cottage.

"Brrt?" Annie ran to them as they entered the hall.

"A woman was killed, Annie," Zoe announced. "This time outside the hair salon."

"Brrp!" *Not again!*

"Brooke sounded pretty sure it was one of her hair dryers," Zoe said.

"Yes, she did, didn't she?"

"But how could she be so sure? She only took a one second look."

"Why would she want to take a longer look?" Lauren asked. She certainly hadn't wanted to gaze at the murder scene any more than she had to.

"She hasn't had the salon long. How many of the hair dryers has she actually used since she bought the place?"

"I have no idea."

"So, what if the hair dryer is from the

batch that Sandra, the former owner, sold to her friends? If she sold Brooke the same type of hair dryers it makes Brooke an obvious suspect."

"Maybe that's what someone wants us to think. That Brooke is the killer." Lauren flopped on the sofa. *So much better.*

"I think I'll have a honey and lemon drink too," Zoe announced. "And then we can talk some more about the murder."

Lauren nodded, pulling a navy throw over her lap.

"Brrp." Annie jumped into her lap, turned around twice, then settled down with a contented sigh.

"I know the feeling," Lauren whispered, surprised her irritated throat let her get the words out.

She was almost asleep when Zoe returned.

"Here."

She blinked her eyes open to see a steaming mug in front of her.

"Thanks." She sipped it gratefully.

"Mm, this is really good." Zoe plopped down on the armchair opposite. "Maybe we should offer these at the café."

"Good idea." Lauren relaxed against the sofa cushions, the warm beverage reviving her.

"So," Zoe began, putting down her mug on the coffee table. "Who wanted to kill Paula?"

Lauren's mind was blank apart from one obvious thought.

"Someone with a hair dryer."

"Yes!" Zoe pointed at her. "Which means it could be anyone. Practically everyone has a hair dryer like that. I do. And you do."

"Mm-hm."

"Although," Zoe pondered, "mine is gray, whereas this one was black."

"Mine is white," Lauren said.

Annie continued to snuggle in Lauren's lap, but now her eyes were open. Lauren was sure the silver-gray tabby was taking in every word.

"I guess the police will check to see if a hair dryer is missing from Brooke's salon," Lauren said.

"They should." Zoe nodded vigorously. "And don't forget what Mrs. Finch said about Sandra selling a load of hair dryers when she decided to retire and sell the salon to Brooke."

"You're right."

"We can ask Mitch if the police have checked for a missing hair dryer, and if they haven't, we'll tell him to check that out."

"I'm sure the police will think of it." Lauren took another sip of her drink. The lemon and honey goodness was definitely helping with her throat.

"So who else wanted to kill Paula?" Zoe frowned. "She didn't seem to be a nice person."

"Maybe she was having a bad day." Lauren tried to be fair.

"Two bad days," Zoe countered. "When we saw her in the salon raging that her perm was ruined because she washed it too soon, and then on Saturday when she came into the café with her friend. And didn't leave a tip."

"That's right."

"But we don't know who Paula was," Zoe said. "Do you think she was new to town?"

Lauren shrugged.

"Maybe we should ask around and find out."

"Or maybe we should leave it to the police." Lauren had the sinking feeling that she'd said that a few times last year – not that it had had any effect.

"Your voice sounds worse," Zoe observed.

"Thanks," Lauren croaked.

"I think you should go to bed. I'll run to the store and get some supplies – juice, et cetera, and you take it easy."

"Thanks," Lauren said gratefully.

"And when I return, we can talk some more about the murder!"

***

As soon as Lauren crawled into bed, her clothes on, she fell asleep, Annie nestled by her side. When she woke, for a moment she had no idea what time it was. Had she slept the whole day away? Or was it only a couple of hours?

She checked her practical white plastic watch. She'd only slept for one hour.

"Are you awake?" she whispered to Annie.

"Brrp?" Annie said sleepily, one eyelid lifting.

"Go back to sleep," she said gently.

Taking her own advice, she closed her eyes and drifted off.

"I think she's asleep," Zoe's whisper filtered through her uneasy doze.

"I don't want to wake her." A masculine voice.

Mitch?

She woke with a start.

"Don't look at me," she croaked, covering her face with her palms.

"She *is* awake," Zoe sounded pleased.

"Are you okay, Lauren?" Mitch's voice was full of concern.

"It's just a cold." Lauren's voice was muffled behind her hands. "But Zoe says I don't look too good."

"I'll be the judge of that." There was a trace of amusement in his voice.

"I'll leave you two alone." Zoe left the room.

"Let me see." Mitch's voice was gentle.

Lauren hesitated, then slowly lowered her hands. She knew she didn't look good when she was sick.

"You still look beautiful to me." His expression was sincere.

"My nose feels big and red," she confessed hoarsely.

"It is a bit," he admitted.

"And I don't have much of a voice right now."

"Then I want you to rest it." He sat down on the side of the bed and took her hand.

"I might infect you," she warned. "Like the sneezing man at the restaurant infected me."

"I'm fine." He smiled at her. "Take plenty of vitamins and drink lots of juice."

"I will. I think we'll have to cancel our plans for Wednesday night," she said regretfully, stroking the necklace he'd given her Saturday night and which she'd worn constantly since.

"I think so, too," he said gently.

"Brrp," Annie agreed. She hadn't left Lauren's side.

"I heard that you were caught up in another murder," Mitch told them. "I wanted to check you were okay."

"I am. Apart from this cold."

"You'd better stay home tomorrow," he said.

Lauren nodded glumly. "But how will Zoe cope on her own?"

"I have a feeling she'll be fine," Mitch told her.

Lauren leaned back against the pillows, knowing he was right. Her cousin was bright, smart, and capable. She could totally handle the café on her own. Unless they were super slammed with customers. But with the cold weather, that probably wouldn't happen.

She started upright.

"The cupcakes," she croaked. "I was going to make up the batter this afternoon—"

"Lie back and rest," he soothed her. "I'll speak to Zoe. Maybe she can make them, or else Ed might be able to work extra hours tomorrow and make more pastries?"

She pressed his hand and nodded. Why hadn't she thought of that? Her brain felt like it was stuffed with cotton wool. She hadn't been like that this morning when she'd woken up.

Mitch stayed with her for a few more minutes, then said goodbye to her and Annie.

"Brrp." Annie nestled even closer to Lauren and closed her eyes.

"I feel the same way," Lauren told her, thinking about Mitch as she dozed off.

***

"I'll be fine on my own today," Zoe assured her the next morning. Lauren lay in bed, propped up against the pillows, Annie beside her. "I'd called Ed while Mitch was visiting you yesterday. He's in the café right now, making extra Danish pastries, including his new one, honeyed walnut."

"Sounds good," Lauren said hoarsely. She shouldn't have doubted Zoe could handle things.

"I'll save us both one." She grinned. "I bet they're going to be his new bestseller, although I'm sure everyone will ask about your cupcakes today." She snapped her fingers. "Maybe I should make a sign and put it on the counter. *No cupcakes today because Lauren is sick. But Ed has a new pastry he wants you to try.*"

Zoe's enthusiasm brought a smile to Lauren's face.

"Ooh, I know! I could cut up one of his new pastries and offer it to the customers as a free sample. I bet they'll gobble it up, and want to buy one for themselves." She frowned. "But if I do that, all the honeyed walnuts will go as freebies because everyone will want to try one."

"Limited time offer," Lauren croaked. "Only cut up two pastries."

"Why didn't I think of that?" Zoe winked. "You're going to be better in no time. I just know it!"

Zoe left for the café earlier than usual, since she would have to do all the setting up herself.

"Brrt?" Annie asked once they were alone.

"I'm not going to the café today because I'm sick," Lauren told her. "But you can go and keep Zoe company if you like, and show the customers to their tables as usual."

"Brrp." Annie climbed into Lauren's lap for a snuggle.

Lauren stroked her velvet soft fur, the soothing motion lulling her to sleep. When she woke a couple of hours later, Annie was no longer there.

"Annie?" she called out as loudly as she could.

There was no answer. The feline must be at the café.

Lauren managed to get out of bed, and decided to take a shower. Zoe had offered her breakfast earlier, but she'd had no appetite. Right now, food didn't appeal to her at all.

She felt a little better after her shower, and put on fresh clothes. Maybe she could work on her hat if she felt up to it. As soon as she sat down on the sofa, a coughing attack shook her. Great.

A jug of orange juice with an accompanying glass was on the coffee table. Zoe. She was so lucky. Lauren poured herself some and told herself to drink it all, the juice a welcome contrast to her hot, sore throat, although she noticed it didn't seem quite so irritated right now.

"Brrt?" Annie trotted into the living room.

"I thought I'd sit in here," Lauren told her.

"Brrt!" Annie sounded as if she approved.

"What have you been up to?"

"Brrp." Annie jumped up next to her.

"How's Zoe managing in the café? Did you go to see her?"

"Brrt." *Yes.* Annie pushed a cell phone toward Lauren.

"My phone." Lauren had wondered if she'd left it in her purse, then couldn't be bothered to think about it again.

"Brrt." Annie patted the buttons with her paw.

"You want me to call Zoe?"

"Brrp." *Yes.*

"I don't want to bother her if she's busy."

Annie pressed three buttons with her paw. The phone vibrated to life.

"All right." Lauren dialed Zoe.

"Brrp." Annie very delicately pressed a button on the phone.

Lauren peered at the icon, then smiled. She and Zoe had recently installed video apps on their devices, but hadn't had a chance to use them yet.

"Let's see if it works." She marveled at Annie's ingenuity.

"Lauren?" The side of Zoe's face came into view; her pixie bangs a little askew

79

as she foamed milk and spoke into the phone at the same time. "Are you okay?"

"I'm fine." Lauren held the phone toward her and Annie, hoping her cousin could see them. "Look."

"Awesome, you're on the sofa." Zoe grinned. "Hi, Annie. She was in here a little while ago, seating customers, then wanted to go home to you."

"Thank you." Lauren gently patted the cat. "How are you doing, Zoe?"

"Good," she replied. "It's not too busy yet. Ed's pastries are a big hit so far, so don't worry." The low hum of conversation in the background punctuated her words. "Drink all the juice I left you."

"I'll try." Lauren disconnected the call and turned to Annie. "That was a great idea, using the video app."

"Brrt," Annie said proudly. She snuggled next to Lauren.

Lauren spent the rest of the morning watching TV and knitting her hat. Annie spent the rest of the morning alternating between visiting Zoe at the café, and visiting Lauren on the sofa.

Zoe dashed in at lunchtime with a

panini and one of Ed's new pastries, then dashed back to the café, saying she'd eat her lunch between customers.

Lauren felt a little better in the afternoon and tried the new pastry – delicious, even with a cold. She was sure Zoe would say it was all that orange juice working – but was glad she hadn't attempted to work in the café that day. Hopefully tomorrow she'd be back to normal.

***

Lauren was even worse the next day.

"Not enough juice – or vitamins," Zoe scolded.

Lauren thought she would turn into a large orange if she drank any more OJ.

"Mm." She mopped her streaming nose. Then coughed. "Don't let me infect you."

"I won't," Zoe said airily. She stood a good distance away from Lauren's bed. "You'd better stay in bed all day. I'll be fine. Ed said he can come in early again today and everyone understood that you couldn't make cupcakes when you're sick. I suppose I could try making the cupcakes," Zoe mused, "but they won't be as good as yours."

"Ed," Lauren croaked.

"Okay," Zoe acquiesced. "Ed's pastries only."

"Mrs. Finch?" Lauren managed.

"She came in yesterday." When Zoe had closed the café at five o'clock yesterday, she'd been bushed, and hadn't been as talkative as usual.

"Paula?" Lauren asked.

"No news." Zoe shook her head. "Although a detective did come by the café yesterday and asked me some questions – not Mitch," she added. "He wanted to see you, but I told him you had a very bad cold and might be infectious. You should have seen his face." She laughed. "Men can be such babies."

"Not Mitch."

"No, not Mitch," Zoe said, her tone serious. "He's one of the good ones."

Lauren wanted to say, What about Chris? But didn't like to. She had no idea how serious Zoe was about Mitch's friend.

Zoe departed to the café, Annie by her

side. As she scampered through the bedroom door, she turned back to Lauren.

"Brrt." *Back soon.*

Lauren spent the morning knitting her hat – or trying to. She kept making holes, and ripping out her work. With a sigh, she finally put her knitting down and turned on the TV. She didn't feel up to reading.

She flicked through the channels. Nothing interesting. Looking at her watch, she discovered it was noon. Annie hadn't come back, either. Maybe Mrs. Finch was at the café and Annie was keeping her company?

Lauren reached for her phone and turned it on. It vibrated in her hand.

"Hi, Zoe." She'd pressed the video app. "How are things?"

Zoe's face came into view. There was a smudge of what looked like chocolate powder on her cheek as she stood behind the counter, plating a blueberry Danish.

"Everything's good." She grinned. "We're pretty busy. That's why Annie hasn't gone home. Customers keep coming in and she shows them to a table."

"What's she doing right now?" Lauren asked curiously.

"Sitting with Mrs. Finch." Zoe turned the phone so Lauren had a side view of Annie sitting at Mrs. Finch's table, appearing to listen to the senior.

She'd been right about her keeping Mrs. Finch company.

"Oh, Brooke's here," Zoe told her in a lower tone. "She said since the murder, she's hardly had any customers."

"That's a shame," Lauren sympathized.

"She's having a latte and one of Ed's pastries right now," Zoe added. She looked away from the phone. "Ooh, you'll never guess who's just walked in the door."

"Mitch?"

"No, the flower guy from the salon. Jeff."

Lauren's eyes widened. Zoe maneuvered the phone toward the café door. He wore gray slacks and a mint sweater and stood uncertainly at the *Please Wait to be Seated* sign.

"I don't know if Annie will be able to find somewhere for him to sit," Zoe said into the phone, now holding it toward Mrs. Finch's table.

As if Annie had heard her, she jumped down from her chair and trotted over to Jeff.

"Brrt," she told him, turning around and threading her way through the occupied tables, her plumy silver tail waving in the air.

"Follow her," Zoe advised him.

"Um … okay." He looked bewildered but obeyed.

"Brrt." Annie stopped at Brooke's small table.

The hair stylist looked up from her coffee and smiled. "Oh, hi, Jeff."

"Hi." He smiled shyly.

Brooke noticed Annie. "Hi, Annie."

"Brrt." Annie looked at the empty chair at Brooke's table.

"You want me to sit here?" Jeff furrowed his brow.

Brooke looked around the packed café. "It's okay with me. I was pretty lucky to get this table."

"Thanks." He lowered himself into the vacant chair.

Annie seemed to nod slightly, then

headed back to Mrs. Finch.

Zoe zipped over to Brooke and Jeff's table.

"Hi, guys." She held the phone so Lauren could see the couple up close. They looked a little surprised at Zoe's appearance.

"Hi," Brooke replied. She peered at the phone. "Is that Lauren?"

"Hi." Lauren waved, wondering what her cousin was up to.

"I can take your order, Jeff," Zoe said.

"You look very busy." He scanned the room. "Brooke says I should go over to the counter to order."

"She's right, but I thought I'd save you the trouble." Zoe beamed.

Uh oh. Lauren had a sinking feeling Zoe was up to something.

"We've been talking about Paula's murder." Zoe waggled the phone. "Where were you at the time of Paula's death?"

Jeff looked like she'd suddenly shone a flashlight in his face. "Um … I was delivering flowers. To Rhonda!" he gabbled.

"Who's Rhonda?" Zoe frowned.

"A friend of Paula's." His eyebrows

scrunched, as if he was thinking. "She was in the salon that day when Paula stormed in about her hair."

"Huh. Was she under the hair dryer?"

"Yeah." He nodded. "And that's what I was doing. Delivering flowers to Rhonda."

"Zoe!" A customer waved to her from the other side of the room.

"Excuse me, guys." Zoe strode toward the calling customer. "Did you see that?" Zoe spoke into the phone. "Did you hear what Jeff said?"

"Yes," Lauren replied, sitting back against the sofa cushions. "Interesting."

"We'll have to discuss it later," Zoe told her. "But I think she likes him."

"Who? Annie likes Jeff?"

"No, Brooke likes Jeff. And I think he likes her."

"How do you know?"

"It's just a feeling." Zoe waved her hand. "Didn't you notice the two of them checking each other out when he delivered flowers to her at the salon?"

"That's right," she agreed. "They did."

"And Jeff was Paula's ex-husband."

Lauren nodded, hoping Zoe could see

her do that.

"I guess he doesn't have to worry about her making trouble for him."

"Zoe!"

"Sorry." Zoe grimaced. "I'm just thinking out loud. I miss you being here, but Annie is a great help."

"I miss being there, too." Lauren coughed.

"Are you taking your vitamins?"

"Yes."

"And did you drink all the juice I left you?"

"Not quite." Lauren quickly poured herself a glass and raised it to her lips. "See? I'm going to take a big mouthful right now."

"Good."

They ended the call as Zoe hurried to the customer's table.

Lauren closed her eyes for a few minutes. That was interesting about Jeff and Brooke. Or was it? Surely they didn't have anything to do with the murder?

Wasn't the spouse one of the first suspects? But Jeff was the *ex*-husband of Paula. Why would he want to kill her? Although, he had looked a bit nervous when Zoe interrogated him.

She told herself to think of something nicer, like new cupcake flavors. Lauren enjoyed coming up with ideas, and now was the perfect time to dream up a new creation, when she couldn't do much else.

She ran through the current offerings: triple chocolate ganache, vanilla, raspberry swirl, cinnamon swirl, blueberry, orange poppyseed, Norwegian Apple cake, white chocolate cherry.

Lavender. The idea popped into her mind. She'd recently read an article about using culinary lavender in cakes.

The more she thought about it, the more excited she became. She grabbed a notepad from the kitchen. What if she could use actual lavender flowers for a decoration? Edible ones, of course.

"Brrt?" Annie ran into the living room and jumped up on the sofa next to Lauren.

"I'm writing down ideas for a new cupcake." Lauren showed her the page.

"Brrt!" Annie sounded as if she approved.

"What have you been up to?" Lauren

asked. "I saw you sitting with Mrs. Finch." She pointed to the phone and smiled. "I used the video app again."

"Brrt." *Good.*

Annie climbed onto her lap and turned around in a circle.

Lauren realized with a start that she wasn't feeling quite so bad. Perhaps it was thinking about cupcakes, connecting with Zoe and the happenings at the café over the phone, or having Annie in her lap, but Lauren felt more cheerful.

CHAPTER 5

"I'm nearly better," Lauren protested the following day while they ate breakfast. She coughed.

"*Nearly.*" Zoe shook her head. "Annie and I can cope. And Ed."

"I know." Zoe had done a wonderful job the last two days.

"You don't want to sneeze over the coffee or the pastries," Zoe continued. "And I don't think you're up to baking cupcakes."

"Maybe not," Lauren replied ruefully, an idea forming in her mind.

"I've got to go." Zoe scraped back her chair. "Everyone loved Ed's honeyed walnut pastries and he said he'd come in early again today and make extra. I'm even thinking of putting the price up by ten cents since they're such a hit."

"Good thinking." Lauren stirred her oatmeal. Her appetite had come back a little, but she wasn't up to crunching on granola. She didn't think she wanted any more oatmeal this morning, either.

"Oh, Brooke and I spoke about the murder a bit yesterday before Jeff shared her table. She said she was late opening the salon on Monday because her mom called just as she was leaving."

"Did she tell the police that?" Lauren asked.

"Brrt?" Annie's ears pricked. She sat next to Lauren at the kitchen table.

"She said she did," Zoe replied. "I like Brooke. I don't want her to be the killer."

"Me, neither," Lauren replied. "I guess the police will be able to trace the phone call. What about Jeff? Does his alibi check out?"

"I haven't heard anything either way." Zoe frowned. "If the detective on the case knows he's in the clear, he hasn't shared that with me." She sounded a bit put out.

They didn't know the detective, so Lauren wasn't surprised he hadn't given Zoe an update on the case.

Zoe zoomed off to the café, Annie electing to stay with Lauren for the time being.

"I think we should order some culinary lavender," Lauren told the cat.

"Brrt!"

Annie followed Lauren to the living room, where the laptop lay on the coffee table.

After a few minutes, Lauren closed the device. "Hopefully it will arrive next week," she told Annie. *And hopefully I'll be all better by then.*

Annie spent the morning trotting back and forth from the cottage to the café.

"I might not be able to go to Mrs. Finch's for club night tomorrow," Lauren told Annie at lunchtime. "I don't want to give her my cold." That morning she'd been convinced she was getting better, but now, halfway through the day, her cold seemed to have freshened up a little. "Maybe I need to take more vitamins."

"Brrt." Annie sounded approving.

Lauren took some vitamin C and flopped down on the sofa. Should she call Zoe? She didn't want to bother her if she was busy serving customers, but maybe it wasn't so busy today if Annie was with her in the cottage?

She gave in to temptation.

"What's up?" Zoe smiled at her through the phone. She stood behind the counter.

"How is everything?" Lauren asked.

"It's slower today so far," Zoe told her.

"Everyone's asking about you and when you're coming back."

"That's nice." Lauren was cheered.

"Hans is here." Zoe picked up the phone and headed toward a table near the front. "Hans, Lauren is on the phone." She handed the device to the dapper man in his sixties.

"Hi, Hans." Lauren cleared her throat.

"Hello, Lauren," Hans replied. "It is no good that you are sick."

"I think I'm getting better," Lauren told him.

"That is *gut*." He beamed, his faded blue eyes looking kindly. "Is Annie keeping you company?"

"Brrt!" Annie peered at the phone when she heard Hans' voice.

"I see you, *Liebchen*," he said to her.

"Brrt." *Good.*

Hans wished her a speedy recovery, then handed the phone back to Zoe.

"Everything's under control," her cousin assured her. "But – Ms. Tobin has just walked in."

"Oh," Lauren replied. Ms. Tobin used to be their prickliest customer, but after they had warned her she was being scammed online, Ms. Tobin had mellowed a little.

"I'll explain to her that Annie is with you right now," Zoe said.

Zoe must have moved her hand because now all Lauren could see was her denim jeans.

"Hi, Ms. Tobin," Zoe said perkily.

"Hello, Zoe." A pause. "Where is Annie? She always greets me."

"Oh – I forgot to hold the phone up."

Lauren could now see Ms. Tobin, a tall, slender woman in her fifties standing at the *Please Wait to be Seated* sign. Today she wore fawn pants and an amber sweater which complimented her brown hair.

"Annie's on the phone. Look." Zoe held up the phone so the other woman could see.

"Hi, Ms. Tobin," Lauren called on the other end, hoping she didn't look too dreadful.

"Brrt!" *Hello!*

"Lauren, what are you doing?" Ms. Tobin sounded more puzzled than scolding. "Annie, are you all right, dear?"

"She's fine," Zoe assured her. "Lauren

has a cold, and Annie is keeping her company right now. I think she's getting better, though."

"Well, that is good news," Ms. Tobin replied. She paused. "Does that mean you're here on your own, Zoe?"

"Don't worry, I can manage," Zoe told her. "Ed's in the kitchen making extra Danishes, because there aren't any cupcakes."

"Oh." Ms. Tobin sounded disappointed.

"Ed has made this amazing new pastry, though," Zoe told her. "You must try it. It's sold out each day this week."

"Very well," Ms. Tobin replied. "Thank you."

"Sit anywhere you like," Zoe said.

"Annie, where do you think I should sit?" Ms. Tobin looked directly into the phone screen.

"Brrt!" Annie peered back at her.

"Good idea." Zoe sounded amused. She held the phone out so Ms. Tobin and Annie could see each other as they walked toward the tables. "Tell us when to stop, Annie."

After passing a four-seater and a six-seater, they approached a two-seater table not too far from the counter.

"Brrt." *Sit here.*

"Thank you, Annie." Ms. Tobin pulled out a chair.

"What would you like with your honeyed walnut pastry?" Zoe asked. "Your usual large latte?"

"That would be perfect, Zoe. Thank you," Ms. Tobin replied.

Zoe and her phone departed to the counter. "I'll see you later," she told Lauren. "I want to make a good peacock on this latte."

"I understand," Lauren replied. They waved goodbye to each other before ending the call, Annie lifting a paw as well. Although Ms. Tobin had mellowed recently, she could still be particular about how her latte was made.

Lauren heated up some soup for her lunch, while Annie enjoyed chicken in gravy. She hoped Zoe had time to eat something between customers. Usually they spelled each other at lunch, either grabbing a meal here in the cottage, or buying something locally.

Annie departed to the café that

afternoon, bringing Zoe home with her after five.

"Today was good." Zoe flopped on the sofa beside Lauren. "Not too many customers." She looked guilty for a second. "I shouldn't be happy about that."

"It's totally understandable," Lauren told her. "How did Ms. Tobin like the honeyed walnut pastry?"

"She loved it." Zoe grinned. "And bought another one to take home!"

CHAPTER 6

The following week, Lauren felt a lot better. She'd stayed home Friday night instead of accompanying Zoe and Annie to craft club at Mrs. Finch's. She didn't want to give their elderly friend her cold.

Mitch had called her every evening, checking to see how she was. He'd also visited a couple of times, bringing soup for her, teasing that Zoe had the juice angle covered. And whenever she spoke to him, she always traced her finger over her necklace. She hadn't taken it off since he'd given it to her, except to shower.

She'd insisted the café stay closed Saturday morning, in order to give Zoe a break. Besides, Ed didn't work Saturdays, even though he'd offered to on this occasion. But he'd already worked extra hours that week, baking more pastries to make up for the lack of cupcakes.

Zoe insisted Lauren rest on the weekend, taking her own advice as well.

"Maybe you'll be all better by Tuesday." She eyed Lauren hopefully.

"I'd better be," Lauren joked,

determined that would be the case.

And on Tuesday, she crunched her granola at breakfast, and left with Annie and Zoe to open the café. The only thing she hadn't done was mix up batches of cupcakes.

"You can do that this afternoon," Zoe told her as they entered the café, "like you usually do. Ed said he'd come in early today and make extra Danishes."

"Thanks," Lauren said gratefully. She didn't know what she would have done without Zoe and Ed to keep the place running.

She looked around, noting that the pale yellow walls looked exactly the same – not that she'd expected anything else.

They unstacked the pine chairs, Annie 'supervising' by sitting in her pink cat bed.

"Now everything's back to normal," Zoe said with satisfaction, "apart from finding Paula's killer."

"You mean the police haven't made an arrest?" Lauren stared at her cousin. She'd been busy feeling miserable last week, and had tried not to think too much about the murder – especially when she'd been home alone.

"Nope." Zoe shook her head.

"No one came to question me." Lauren remembered Zoe had mentioned a detective taking her statement.

"I think he was worried he'd catch your cold." Zoe laughed. "Or, maybe he doesn't need to ask you anything," she mused. "You should check with Mitch when you see him."

"I will," Lauren replied, counting how many days it had been since he'd visited her at the cottage with some soup.

"Want a latte before we open?" Zoe asked her.

"I'd love one." Her mouth watered at the thought. She hadn't felt like coffee last week, and there'd been no time at breakfast to make one for herself.

Lauren could hear baking trays rattling away in the kitchen, a sign Ed had arrived and was busy making his tender, flaky pastries.

She watched Zoe pour more coffee beans into the hopper, and press the button to grind enough for an espresso.

Frowning, she peered at Zoe's finger.

"Your finger looks a bit strange." Her

cousin's finger pad had small cuts and scratches on it. "Are you okay? Did you hurt it?"

"This?" Zoe stared at her hand, then waved it in the air. "It's nothing. It's just scratches from making the bead jewelry."

"Really?"

"Yeah." Zoe shrugged. "I had no idea that would happen – it must be from working with the wire, even though I try to be careful. I'll have to start putting lotion on them."

"That's a good idea," Lauren said.

"Brrt!" Annie added from her cat bed.

"But," Zoe added as she steamed the milk for the latte, the hissing from the wand punctuating her conversation, "I'm starting to wonder if beading is really for me."

"I thought you liked making bracelets and necklaces." Lauren stared at her. "And I love the one you made me." She felt guilty that she hadn't worn the bangle lately – she was worried it would get in the way when she worked at the café.

"I do – did," Zoe replied. "But having scratched fingers all the time is a bit of a drawback. And how many bangles and necklaces can I wear?"

"So what are you thinking of trying next?" Lauren asked curiously.

"Pottery." Zoe's brown eyes sparkled. "I think I could really sink my hands into that!"

***

Lauren enjoyed her first day back at the café. All their regular customers said they were pleased she was over her cold, although they seemed disappointed there weren't any cupcakes on offer.

Halfway through the morning, a package arrived for her.

"I didn't think there'd be anyone at the cottage, so I came here," the delivery man told Lauren as she signed for the package.

"Thanks." Lauren smiled as she took the small cardboard box from him.

"What is it?" Zoe looked up from the espresso machine.

"Brrt!" Annie looked like she was smiling as she gazed at the box in Lauren's hands.

"You'll see," Lauren teased her cousin.

"Ooh, I bet Annie knows, don't you?" Zoe said to the cat.

"Brrt!" *Yes, I do!*

"It's an idea I came up with last week," Lauren said. "I'm going to try a new cupcake recipe tonight."

"Can't wait!" Zoe's face lit up. "I hope you're giving out samples."

"For us, definitely." Lauren smiled.

She caught up with Mrs. Finch, Hans, and Ms. Tobin, who expressed her pleasure at Lauren – and Annie – being back at the café.

"Although Zoe coped very well on her own," Ms. Tobin told Lauren.

"That's great." Lauren was genuinely pleased about the praise for Zoe.

Just before lunch, Mitch strode into the café. Lauren's heart fluttered.

"Hi." He headed to the counter.

"Hi."

"Brrt?" Annie trotted up to him.

"I don't need a table today, Annie," he told her.

"Brrt." Annie's lower lip jutted out for a second. Then she sighed and ambled back to her cat bed.

"It hasn't been too busy today," Lauren told him. "And Annie had some time off last week when she was keeping me company at home. I think that's why she was eager to find you a table."

"I'm glad you're feeling better." His brown eyes warmed as he studied her.

"So am I."

"The reason I'm here – besides saying hello to my girlfriend – is to let you know that my colleague doesn't think he'll need any extra information from you. He said Zoe's statement was very thorough."

"You mean he's not scared of catching my cold – although I'm over it now?"

"Let's just say he doesn't like getting sick," he replied, hitching a grin.

"How's the case going?" Lauren asked him.

"I'm not working on it, so I can't tell you much. But they're doing everything possible to catch the killer."

"That's good."

"Are you busy Saturday night? I thought we could go out to dinner."

"That would be great," she told him. Then hesitated. "But not that Sacramento restaurant we went to last time, although

I loved it." Especially Mitch giving her the necklace. "Except for the part where that man—"

"I get it," he assured her. "No worries. You pick the place and time."

Lauren chose their favorite bistro located on the outskirts of Gold Leaf Valley, and Mitch promised to pick her up at seven-thirty.

***

That afternoon, a woman who looked familiar came into the café. Annie greeted her at the *Please Wait to be Seated* sign, while Lauren racked her brain. She was sure she'd seen this woman recently. Ash brown locks in a wavy bob, and a plump figure. Today the woman wore black slacks and a fuchsia sweater.

"That's the lady who wants to quilt again," Zoe murmured to her. "Helen."

"Of course!" She turned to Zoe. "She was in here after Brooke fixed my hair—"

"And before you caught your cold," Zoe finished. "She didn't visit last week, though."

"She must be really upset about her friend being killed," Lauren remarked.

"Mm."

They watched as Helen followed Annie to a small table in the middle of the room.

"Thank you," she told Annie, sitting down. She looked pensive for a moment, then studied the menu.

"Maybe we should go over," Lauren whispered to Zoe.

"Good idea."

Lauren scanned the few tables that were occupied. Nobody seemed to need their attention.

"What can we get you?" Lauren asked as they reached Helen's table.

"I would love a latte," the woman said wistfully, "although my friend Paula would have said it's not good for me."

"We're sorry for your loss," Lauren said awkwardly.

"Thank you." The woman gave a little smile. "I remember what you told me about being able to drink six coffees per day. So I think I'll risk a small latte."

"Would you like anything to eat?" Zoe

asked as Lauren wrote down the order.

"Do you have any cupcakes like last time I was here?" the woman's face brightened. "The cinnamon swirl was delicious."

They explained how it was Lauren's first day back at work.

"But there will definitely be cupcakes tomorrow," Lauren assured her.

"I'll try to come in again then."

Zoe sold Helen on Ed's new pastry, and the duo headed back to the counter.

A woman in her forties, with big wavy brunette hair, bustled into the café, spotted Helen and waved. She ignored the *Please Wait to be Seated* sign and rushed over to Helen's table, shrugging off her red coat.

Lauren watched the ladies greet each other as Zoe made the coffee.

"Do you think she'll come over to order?" Lauren asked.

"Nope." Zoe shook her head. "I think she's too busy talking to her friend."

Lauren furrowed her brow. "Wasn't she at the salon that day as well when I had my hair trimmed? I think she was under the big hair dryer."

"Yep, that's Rhonda. Now all we need is Brooke and Jeff, and everyone at the salon when Paula came in demanding Brooke fix her perm would be here."

They stared at each other.

Lauren couldn't help glancing at the door, as if expecting Brooke or Jeff – or both of them – to suddenly materialize. It didn't happen.

"I'll go." Zoe wiggled the milk jug, creating a swan on the surface of the micro foam.

"I'll come with you." Lauren plated a pastry.

Annie dozed in her cat bed.

The duo approached the two women.

"Latte and honeyed walnut pastry." Zoe carefully placed the latte in front of Helen.

"That looks wonderful." Helen's face lit up at the sight of the latte art. "How clever!"

"Would you like to order?" Lauren asked Rhonda.

After giving her order of a large cappuccino, Rhonda resumed talking with Helen.

"I was watching a show on TV last

night about quilting, and thought about that amazing quilt you made a few years ago. It won first place at the county fair. I wish I could make something like that." She sighed.

"You could, Rhonda," Helen replied. "It's just practice. I made my own designs, but there are plenty of patterns out there you can use, from books, or you can get them for free online."

"You know, my teenage daughter told me recently she thought she'd seen a pattern just like yours for sale on the internet. I told her it couldn't have been the same pattern because I'd heard you given up quilting."

"No, it's not mine." Helen looked puzzled. "And that county fair was a few years ago. It must be similar to mine, that's all. There are plenty of patterns with slight variations, and a lot of people don't want to pay for a pattern, which is why I didn't try selling mine. I didn't think anyone would buy them." She took a sip of her latte. "I spent a lot of time and money on that quilt, and I was so proud of it, even before I won first prize." She sighed. "I did give up quilting for a while, but now I've decided to delve into it again."

"That's wonderful." Her friend beamed.

Lauren and Zoe headed back to the counter. Lauren made the coffee, while Zoe kept up a stream of chatter, filling her in on all the little things that had happened last week that she hadn't had time to tell her about.

Lauren took the cappuccino over to Rhonda, who thanked her before resuming her conversation with Helen.

"I can't wait to sample your new cupcake creation tonight." Zoe grinned as Lauren joined her behind the espresso machine. "Did you realize we haven't eaten cupcakes for a whole week?"

CHAPTER 7

That evening, Lauren and Annie stayed in the kitchen after dinner. Zoe was in the living room, watching a crime drama while making another bracelet.

"Let's get started." Lauren smiled at Annie.

"Brrt!" Annie hopped onto a chair and watched as Lauren got out the mixer and the ingredients required to make cupcakes.

"Here's the lavender." Lauren showed Annie the packets of culinary lavender seeds and lavender sprigs.

Annie watched intently as Lauren whipped up the batter. Last time she'd "helped" with a new recipe for Norwegian Apple cake, Annie had stuck her head into the bowl and gotten batter on her whiskers. This time, however, she seemed to remember what had happened, and didn't attempt to peer into the mixing bowl.

Lauren spooned the batter into the cupcake pan and slid it into the oven.

"I can't wait to try them," she told Annie.

"Me, neither." Zoe appeared in the doorway. "Want a hand doing the dishes?"

"That would be great," Lauren admitted. Maybe making cupcakes tonight had been overdoing it a little, since it was her first day back at the café.

They finished washing the dishes, Annie watching them, before the oven timer dinged.

"Now are you going to tell me what kind they are?" Zoe studied the pan as Lauren got it out of the oven.

"Lavender."

"You haven't made those before." Zoe's brown eyes lit up.

"I hope they work," Lauren admitted.

"Brrt!"

Once the cakes had cooled, Lauren and Zoe dug in.

"Mmm," Zoe mumbled around a mouthful. "And you haven't even put frosting on them."

"I was thinking of fondant icing, with a sprig on top for decoration."

"Genius!"

"Brrt!" Annie patted the package that contained the edible flowers.

Lauren put away the remainder of the cakes, before calling it a night.

"I think we should get up a bit earlier tomorrow," Zoe told her, a secretive look on her face. "I've got something in mind."

Lauren briefly wondered what her cousin was up to before sleep claimed her.

***

Lauren had set the alarm thirty minutes earlier than usual, and struggled for a moment to get up when the buzzer woke her. No edging of sunlight around the corners of her drapes, either.

"Something in mind," Lauren mumbled as she munched on whole-wheat toast at the kitchen table. The only thing she slightly disliked about the café was the early starts. She didn't even want to know what time it was on the kitchen clock. Probably just after seven, and she'd already showered and dressed.

"I thought I could get my hair cut this morning," Zoe announced.

Lauren and Annie stared at her.

"But the café opens at nine-thirty," Lauren reminded her, the piece of toast halfway to her mouth.

"And Brooke opens at nine," Zoe countered. "So, I was thinking, we can get set up first, and then run down to the salon just before nine, and be her first customers!"

"Unless she already has appointments booked," Lauren cautioned.

"She said last week she wasn't getting any clients," Zoe replied. "So I'll be her first one today."

"Okay," Lauren said. "Why not?" She could always race back to the café before nine-thirty if it looked like Zoe was going to be stuck at the salon for a while.

"Thanks, boss." Zoe grinned.

After breakfast, they trooped down the private hallway to the café.

"I'll make some cupcakes," Lauren said, heading into the commercial kitchen.

"I'll get everything ready out here," Zoe told her.

Annie jumped into her pink cat bed, ready to supervise Zoe.

Lauren whipped up vanilla cupcakes,

then her popular triple chocolate ganache creations. She wished she could make the lavender ones this morning, but was worried she wouldn't have enough time since she and Zoe were going to the salon.

You could always stay here and keep making cupcakes, her sensible voice told her.

But Lauren thought it would be nice to see Brooke. And soon Ed would arrive, and he liked having the kitchen to himself.

This afternoon she'd make up the lavender batter so it would be easy to bake them first thing tomorrow.

After the cupcakes came out of the oven, she placed the pan on a wire rack.

The back door opened and Ed clumped into the kitchen.

"Hi Ed," she called out.

"Hi, Lauren." He nodded.

"How's AJ?"

"She's good." A brief smile. "I think she liked her play date with Annie the other weekend."

"She's welcome anytime," Lauren told him. "Annie enjoyed spending time with her."

She told him how she and Zoe were running down to the salon before nine-thirty.

"No problem," he told her. "I'll be here."

"Ready?" Zoe poked her head into the kitchen. "Hi, Ed."

"Hi." He was already pulling out flour and sugar, and placing it on the work table.

Lauren left the kitchen, not wanting to disturb Ed when he was in the zone.

"Let's go."

"What about Annie?" Lauren frowned and looked over at her. The silver-gray tabby sat in her bed, her ears pricked and a questioning look on her face. "Will you be okay here if Zoe and I quickly go to the hair salon and come back by opening time? Or do you want to go back to the cottage?"

"Brrt." Annie turned around in a circle and sank down into the cat bed.

"Annie can mind the café for us." Zoe winked at the cat.

"Brrp!"

"The door will be locked, and Ed is in

the kitchen," Lauren told Annie. "You'll be safe in here."

"Brrt." *I know.*

They hurried down the street to the salon.

"We're sure to be her first customers." Zoe charged ahead.

Lauren struggled to keep up. Maybe she needed to do some more exercise, although after a full day at the café, she didn't feel like doing much, unless it involved knitting, or watching TV with Zoe. *Or going on a date with Mitch.*

Lauren panted as they reached the salon.

"She's open," Zoe crowed, yanking open the door and zipping inside.

"High, high." A familiar blonde toddler clapped her hands as the chair she sat in cranked higher and higher.

"Hi, Zoe, and Lauren." Claire, an athletic woman, greeted them. She had blonde hair like her daughter, and was dressed in pale blue track pants with a matching jacket.

"Zoe! Lauren!" Molly clapped her hands again.

Lauren waved, catching her breath.

"Where Annie?" Molly pouted.

"Minding the café," Lauren managed. Molly giggled.

"Hi." Brooke approached them. Apart from Claire and Molly, they were the only customers in the place.

Zoe explained how she thought she would be the first customer.

"Ordinarily, you would," Brooke confessed. "But I opened a few minutes before nine this morning, and Molly and Claire came in straight away."

"I thought this might be a good time to get Molly's hair cut," Claire explained, "when it would be quiet."

"I understand." Zoe nodded. "I can come back another time."

"Why don't you stay?" Lauren touched her cousin's arm. "I'm sure I can manage on my own for a while. You did last week."

"If you're sure," Zoe said doubtfully.

"Of course I am." She was convinced she was completely over her cold. "I can handle it."

"Okay. Thanks." Zoe grinned.

They all chatted with Brooke as she wrapped a pink cape around Molly.

"I thought those types of hair dryers were old-fashioned." Zoe pointed to the big hooded hair dryer on the opposite side of the salon. "But there was a woman sitting under it when Lauren was here getting a trim – Rhonda."

"They're making a comeback," Brooke told her. "I inherited it from Sandra, the previous owner, when I bought the salon, and thought it a shame to get rid of it. I was a little surprised when one of my first customers requested it, though. But no one has since."

"I'm sure they will," Lauren told her.

Brooke combed Molly's hair.

"Just a little trim," Claire told her.

"Of course." Brooke smiled. She turned to Lauren and Zoe. "By the way, I've arranged a hair appointment with Mrs. Finch at her house."

"Awesome! Brooke cut Lauren's hair," Zoe told Claire.

"That's right." Lauren nodded. "I love it." She patted her hair. Especially after Brooke had saved her from her cousin's trim gone wrong.

"I'll need a haircut in a few weeks," Claire said, watching her daughter. Molly sat still, her eyes big and round as she stared at herself and Brooke in the large mirror.

"Then you must come here," Zoe told her.

"I hope you do," Brooke told Claire. "But it's okay if you prefer going somewhere else. After what happened here last week – with Paula—" she kept her voice low "—I'm surprised I have any customers at all."

"It must be tough to start a business in a new town," Zoe remarked.

Lauren nodded. She'd inherited her grandmother's café and had often come down to visit Gramms and help out, so she'd been a known quantity to the townsfolk when she took over.

"I really want this salon to be successful," Brooke told them. "I didn't have enough savings to buy this place, so my parents lent me the rest of the money. They said it would be better than trying to get a business loan, as I wouldn't be paying interest. But I want to pay them back as soon as possible."

"Of course," Lauren murmured.

Brooke finished cutting Molly's hair.

"That looks perfect." Claire admired her daughter's slightly trimmed locks, the golden curls kept intact. "Thank you."

"Down, down," Molly called, waving her chubby arms in the air.

Brooke whisked the cape off the toddler and cranked down the chair.

"Fank you." Molly beamed at the stylist.

"Thank *you*," Brooke told her, "for sitting so still."

Lauren checked her practical white watch. "I've got to run. It's nearly nine-thirty!"

She made her goodbyes, and jogged down the street, hoping there weren't any customers waiting impatiently.

By the time she reached the cafe, she was out of breath – again. *I must do something about my fitness*, she chided herself. But all thoughts of exercise fled when she saw Mitch standing there.

***

After making Mitch a latte and telling him about their dash to the salon, she watched him stride out of the café, heading to work.

"How many customers do you think we'll get today, Annie?"

"Brrt." *Lots.*

Annie's prediction came true. When Zoe rushed in after her haircut, Lauren already had three orders for coffee.

"Sorry." Zoe joined Lauren behind the counter, her pixie cut looking a little shorter, but bouncier. "What can I do?"

"Plate the cupcakes." Lauren nodded at the orders on the workspace.

The morning passed quickly. They sold out of cupcakes at the end of lunch, as well as Ed's pastries.

Lauren sank down on a stool during a brief lull in the afternoon. Zoe sat on the matching stool, dangling her feet.

"It's as if everyone knew you made cupcakes today." Zoe grinned.

"I should have made more," Lauren chided herself.

"Don't be so hard on yourself."

Although Annie had been correct about lots of customers that morning, the afternoon proved to be a little different. Only two women arrived separately in the next hour, giving Lauren plenty of time to plan tomorrow's cupcake offerings.

The entrance door opened and Jeff walked up to the *Please Wait to be Seated* sign.

"Brrt." Annie ran up to him.

"Okay," he told her.

Annie swiveled and led the way through the empty café, pausing at a four-seater in the middle of the room.

"Brrt," she encouraged.

"Um …thanks." Jeff pulled out a chair and sat down.

Zoe tapped Lauren on the arm. "Look!"

Lauren returned Zoe's tap. "Double look!"

Rhonda stepped into the café.

"Brrt." Annie trotted to greet the newcomer.

"Aren't you cute." Rhonda bent to greet her.

"Brrt." *Yes.*

Annie sashayed through the café, until she reached Jeff's table.

"Brrt."

Lauren raised her eyebrow as she glanced at her cousin. Annie's seating

decision was a tad unusual, especially
since there were plenty of tables to
choose from.

"Huh," Zoe murmured.

Lauren watched Rhonda and Jeff greet
each other. Were they a trifle awkward?
She wasn't sure.

"I'll go over," Zoe stage-whispered.

Lauren accompanied her cousin as
they approached the table.

"I want to thank you once again for
delivering Baxley," Rhonda said to Jeff.
"It can't have been easy for you not
telling anyone, especially after Paula's –
death – but I really appreciate—"

"What can we get you?" Zoe asked in
a chipper voice.

"We can take your orders." Lauren
whipped out her pad.

"Oh – um …" Rhonda tapped a mauve
polished fingernail on the laminated
menu.

"A large latte would be great," Jeff
said.

"I'll have the same," Rhonda said. "Do
you have any cupcakes?"

"They're sold out," Zoe told her. "So
are the pastries."

"That's too bad." Rhonda sighed.

Lauren and Zoe glanced at each other. Annie had departed for her cat bed. Lauren worried that this morning's influx of customers might have tired her out a little.

"It was sad about Paula, wasn't it?" Zoe made conversation. "Did you know her very well, Rhonda?"

Lauren frowned at the interrogation. What was her cousin up to?

"A little," Rhonda admitted. "She could be – I know I shouldn't speak ill of the dead, but she could be a difficult person at times."

"That's for sure," Jeff said morosely. "She cleaned me out in the divorce. Said being a florist wasn't a real job, and I should get it together. It's amazing my lawyer managed to retain the shop for me."

"Have you heard if the police have any new leads?" Zoe pressed. "We haven't, have we, Lauren?"

"No." Lauren shook her head.

"Me neither," Rhonda told them. "But I think there might have been plenty of people who wished they could kill Paula at one time or another."

"Yeah." Jeff nodded. "The police have looked at me pretty hard, but I had an alibi." He swiftly glanced at Rhonda.

"That's right. He was delivering flowers to my—" Rhonda paused, grimacing. "I don't think there's any point lying about it now. The police know the truth."

"Thanks." Relief flitted across Jeff's face.

"Lying about what?" Lauren asked.

"Jeff has an alibi and so do I. But it's not exactly the one he mentioned last week. He told me you asked where he was when Paula was murdered."

"Oh?" Zoe questioned.

"My husband wanted to adopt a dog from the local shelter. I thought it was a great idea, so we visited and fell in love with a beagle mix called Baxley. The shelter checked us out and did a home visit, all the usual things these days when you want to adopt a pet. My husband thought Baxley was arriving after his birthday, but the shelter called me and said we could pick him up a couple of days earlier if we wanted. So I thought it would be fun to surprise him on his birthday with Baxley."

"What was the problem?" Zoe wrinkled her brow.

"The problem was Paula." Rhonda's mouth tightened. "I don't know her as well as Helen does, but when I told her we were adopting, she said she'd been thinking of getting a dog, so why not get one from the shelter? She apparently fell in love with Baxley."

"Oh," Lauren murmured.

"She was furious when she found out that we were already being assessed as suitable owners for him. I don't think she realized that adopting a dog is a bit of a process these days. She even told me that she really wanted Baxley and why didn't I and my husband choose a different dog?"

"No way," Zoe breathed.

"I told her we'd just heard that we were approved to be Baxley's new owners and that it was now going to be a surprise for my husband's birthday. So you know what she did?"

"I don't want to know," Jeff muttered.

"She posted all over social media that

we were adopting Baxley and how happy she was for us." Rhonda snorted. "Yeah, right. She was hoping to ruin my husband's surprise. I'm just lucky he's not into social media, so he didn't see her posts."

"So what did you lie about, Jeff?" Zoe probed.

Jeff flushed. "I was delivering Baxley to Rhonda's house at the time of Paula's murder, not flowers. That's all. I told the police the truth, but ..." he hesitated, "... I had the flower alibi already prepared before I knew Paula was killed. In case one of her friends saw me in Rhonda's neighborhood and reported back to my ex-wife."

"But why would they do that?" Lauren asked.

"To get on her good side," Jeff said. "Not all of them. Not Rhonda, and I always liked Helen – I don't think she would spy on Paula's behalf, although Paula kept borrowing things from her. But even though we were divorced, Paula seemed to like keeping tabs on me."

"Huh." Zoe thought it over. "Like the day we were at the salon and you delivered the flowers to Brooke. Paula wanted to know what you were doing there."

"Exactly." Jeff looked miserable. "The day my divorce was final was the happiest day of my life."

"Paula also borrowed a couple of things from me." Rhonda drummed her fingers on the table. "Like my new hair dryer. It was expensive, too. I never got it back."

"Why did you lend it to her?" Zoe probed.

"She had a way of making you feel that if you didn't do her a favor, you were the meanest person in the world. I'd run into Paula and Helen at the market, and told them about my new hair dryer. Paula said hers had stopped working and she didn't have time to go shopping for a new one, so could she borrow mine because she had a special event the next day. So I lent it to her, and that was the last time I saw it. Whenever I asked her about it, she'd keep making excuses as to why she hadn't returned it. Eventually I stopped asking, but I never forgot about it."

They left Rhonda and Jeff and headed

to the counter.

"I think we're going to have a lot to talk about tonight." Zoe ground the coffee beans into the portafilter.

"Definitely," Lauren agreed.

CHAPTER 8

"I think we should check out Paula's house," Zoe announced that night at dinner.

"What?" Lauren stared at her cousin.

"Brrt?" Annie sat next to Lauren at the kitchen table.

"It makes total sense," Zoe said. "What if the hair dryer used to kill Paula was Rhonda's expensive one?"

"Wouldn't the police have discovered that by now?" Lauren asked.

"Then Rhonda would have been arrested, wouldn't she? Not telling us how Paula practically stole her hair dryer. So if we go to Paula's house, we can see if she has a hair dryer. If she does, and it's a good brand, then we can surmise that Rhonda didn't kill Paula – or at least use her own hair dryer to do it."

"That's breaking and entering." Lauren sounded shocked.

"Not if we can find a key," Zoe replied. "I bet she has a spare key under a rock or something. Ooh, inside a fake rock."

"That still doesn't make it right,"

Lauren told her.

"What if she has some plants that need watering?" Zoe countered. "We could be saving their lives. I bet no one is looking after her house, since it sounds like she made enemies wherever she went."

"I don't think it's a good idea." Lauren shook her head. "Why don't you tell the detective about Rhonda lending her expensive hair dryer to Paula?"

"I already did," Zoe admitted. "Before we closed, when you were mixing up cupcake batter for the morning. He didn't seem to be impressed with my info."

"I'm sorry."

"So." Zoe scraped back her chair. "I'm going to snoop around Paula's house tonight. You can come with me, or stay home. I'll understand if you don't want to go."

"Brrt?" Annie asked.

"I don't think Lauren would let you come with me," Zoe explained.

"That's for sure." Lauren made her voice firm. "You can mind the cottage for us – *if* I decide to go with Zoe." She turned to Annie.

"Brrt." Annie's lower lip pushed out

133

slightly.

***

A few hours later, Lauren found herself accompanying her cousin. It was a dark night, with very few stars out, and the moon was only a quarter sliver.

"I must be mad," she grumbled as she parked the car a few houses down from Paula's. "How do you know where she lived, anyway?"

"I overheard Rhonda and Jeff when we left them to their coffee this afternoon," Zoe said. "I wasn't even trying to eavesdrop – it just happened. Jeff said he didn't know what was going to happen to the house, even though Paula got it in the divorce. Apparently she was an only child, and her parents moved to Costa Rica when they retired so their social security would go further."

"Is he going to contact them?" Lauren asked.

"He told Rhonda the police were handling all that."

"So her parents couldn't be the killers," Lauren assumed.

"Not unless they zipped over here and zipped straight back. But there would be a record of their flight details and their passports," Zoe said.

"Are you sure you want to do this?" Lauren glanced down at her outfit. Black sweater, black pants, even a black beret that Zoe had found in her closet. Blue disposable gloves and white sneakers ruined the monochromatic sleuthing attire.

"Yes," Zoe insisted, glancing down at her own onyx outfit of jeans, sweater, sneakers, and beanie. "I think our snooping makes a difference. We've helped catch four murderers so far."

"And nearly got hurt ourselves," Lauren said ruefully.

"This time will be different," Zoe told her. "All we have to do is sneak into Paula's house, check for hair dryers, and sneak back out."

"Only if we find a key," Lauren cautioned. "We are *not* breaking and entering."

"Okay." Zoe sighed. "I guess if we did that, it might put a crimp in your relationship with Mitch."

"Maybe." She hadn't even thought of that. What would Mitch's reaction be if she was locked up in jail? Would he bail her out? Or deny knowing her? Even as that last thought flitted through her mind, she knew Mitch would never do that. He would definitely bail her out. But after that? She hoped their relationship would never have to go there.

They climbed out of the car and walked down the street. Lights winked from some of the houses. Others were in complete darkness.

"People must go to bed early around here," Zoe murmured.

"It's nearly eleven." Lauren glanced at her watch.

"It won't take long," Zoe assured her. "In and out."

"Were you a cat burglar in a previous life?"

"No, but it's an intriguing thought." Zoe grinned. Lauren made out her features under the streetlamp they'd just passed.

"Here." Zoe tapped her arm a few seconds later. She led the way up the driveway until they were at the side of the small Victorian house. "She might have had a key for the back door."

"What about for the front door?"

"We might look conspicuous," Zoe whispered.

Lauren raised an eyebrow, but followed her cousin's lead, looking around for a rock that could be covering up a key.

Zoe dug out her phone and turned on the flashlight app.

"Look!" She pointed to a brown rock. Turning it over, she groaned with disappointment. "No."

"Wouldn't the key be near the back door? Not along the side of the house?"

"You look there, then. I'll keep checking for one here." Zoe waved a hand toward the rear.

Lauren tiptoed along the drive, feeling a mite silly. Were they really doing the right thing by checking out Paula's house? Or: entering Paula's house without permission? But when Zoe had an impulse, it could be hard to dissuade her. And Zoe's theory had made Lauren curious – had Paula been strangled by Rhonda's expensive hair dryer? Or by someone else's?

Lauren turned over a rock near the back door. Nothing. Then she froze. A faint jingle sounded from it. Her eyes widened. Had Zoe been correct when she'd surmised that Paula might have a spare key hidden in a faux stone?

Lauren picked it up and studied it. She shook it. *Jingle.* She aimed the flashlight on her phone at the rock and turned it over. There was white plastic backing on it.

She pulled it open, and shook out the key into her palm.

"Zoe!" she hissed. "I've found it!"

"What?" Zoe raced over. Her voice was the only sound apart from a faint car engine in the distance.

Lauren held out the house key.

"Yes!" Zoe charged toward the back door.

"Shh!"

Lauren watched her cousin insert the key into the lock. The door opened.

"Come on!" Zoe beckoned to Lauren.

"What about an alarm?" Lauren asked.

"Pooh." Zoe grimaced. "I didn't think of that." She glanced around. "But nothing's gone off."

"What if it's a silent one?"

"Then we should hurry!"

Against her better judgment, Lauren followed her cousin into the house. They found Paula's bedroom at the front of the dwelling. Zoe crossed to the windows and pulled the drapes.

"Turn on the light," she ordered.

Lauren did so. The décor was cream and gold with a few fancy pink cushions on the bed. "I hope no one can see us in here."

"The hair dryer might be in the bathroom." Zoe rifled through a dresser drawer. "Nope, not in here." She took out a photo frame and studied it. "Look."

"What is it?" Lauren peered over her shoulder. "A picture of Jeff and Paula."

"Look at how Paula is smiling." Zoe tapped a gloved finger at the dead woman's face. "And she's holding out her hand. Oh, she's showing off her wedding ring – and her engagement ring."

Lauren stared at the photo. Jeff and Paula stood in a garden, surrounded by roses. Paula's outstretched hand showed a large diamond ring and a gleaming gold band. She wore a fancy cream dress, while Jeff wore a smart suit.

"Do you think that's their wedding photo?"

"Could be. But look at the expression on his face," Zoe observed. "He's staring into the distance and has that *how did this happen* expression on his face that men have sometimes."

"Like he has no idea how he came to be married to Paula," Lauren murmured.

"Exactly. Paula must have trapped him into marriage."

"Trapped him?" Lauren looked at her cousin. "How would she do that?"

"The usual ways," Zoe told her.

"Which are?"

"You know." Zoe mimed a baby bump.

"But they don't have kids. Do they?"

"No." Zoe shook her head. "Because surely Jeff would have mentioned it at the café – or Paula's friends would have said something about her child straight after her death." She tapped her cheek. "Maybe we'd better find out for sure that they were childless."

"Good idea."

"Or maybe she seduced him," Zoe pondered. "I bet if Paula put her mind to it, Jeff wouldn't have known what had hit him – until it was too late. Yeah, I bet that was it." She replaced the photo in the drawer.

"What if that gives him a motive for murder?" Lauren suggested. "He realized too late he was stuck in a marriage he didn't want. He said at the café that it was a bitter divorce. Maybe he got fed up with the whole thing and killed her."

"But wouldn't he have killed her before the divorce? That way he would have gotten everything."

"Maybe he hoped it would be amicable? And realized too late it wasn't going to be. And if he killed Paula in the middle of it, he would be the prime suspect."

"Good point." Zoe pointed at her. "That makes a lot of sense."

"Thanks."

Zoe opened another drawer. "No hair dryer in here, either."

"What about the closet?" Lauren opened the door and stared at the racks of shirts, skirts, and jeans. She looked down at the floor. "No."

"You keep searching in here and I'll check out the bathroom." Zoe hurried out of the room.

Lauren had a sinking feeling she shouldn't have agreed to this – in fact, she should have talked her cousin out of the idea. What if they got caught? Who would look after Annie if they were in jail?

She turned off the bedroom light, drew back the drapes, and went to find Zoe, ready to tell her they needed to get out of there now, with or without finding the hair dryer, when she heard a muffled shriek.

"Found it!"

Zoe stood in the bathroom doorway, brandishing a large, black hair dryer. "Rhonda was right, it is expensive. I was looking at these online a few months ago but I didn't want to pay so much."

"So Rhonda didn't strangle Paula." Now they could get out of there.

"Not with this thing, anyway."

"Put it back and let's go," Lauren ordered.

Zoe raised her eyebrows at the bossy tone, but obeyed.

"Good thing we wore gloves," Zoe said in satisfaction as she followed Lauren down the hall and toward the back door. "No fingerprints."

"Maybe you really were a cat burglar in a previous life," Lauren murmured.

"Yeah."

They returned the key to the fake rock and walked back down the driveway.

"Act natural," Zoe instructed. "We're just on a night-time stroll."

"Wearing these?" Lauren held out her blue gloved hand.

"Take them off." Zoe halted and pulled off her black gloves, stuffing them into her pocket. "There. Now we are completely innocent and natural."

"Mm-hm," Lauren murmured skeptically, copying her cousin's movements.

They were only a few steps away from the car when a vehicle drove past them, stopped, then parked a few feet away.

Lauren and Zoe looked at each other. What—?

"Lauren." Mitch swiftly exited the car

and strode toward her and Zoe. "What are you doing here?"

"What are *you* doing here?" Zoe countered, standing tall. "We're just out for an evening walk."

Lauren stared at her boyfriend, all thought fleeing. It looked like their relationship had just gone "there", or closer to "there" than she would have liked.

"Lauren?" Mitch prompted.

She was sure she looked like a deer in the headlights – or an apprentice to Zoe's cat burglar but without a clue.

"You wouldn't be visiting Paula's house, would you?" he asked.

"I ... I thought you weren't working the case," Lauren managed.

"I'm not. But this case is being discussed a lot in the office."

"If you're not on the case, what are you doing here?" Zoe challenged Mitch.

"I was driving home from a buddy's place, minding my own business," he countered, frowning, "when I saw my girlfriend and her cousin near the victim's house late at night."

"Huh," Zoe muttered.

"We're going home," Lauren managed.

"Good." Mitch nodded. "I'll follow you."

"Good." Lauren smiled tentatively.

She got into the car, her hands shaking as she clenched the steering wheel.

"It's okay," Zoe told her. "He didn't suspect a thing – well, okay, he did. But I'm sure we didn't commit a crime – we found the spare key – and we didn't steal anything."

"We are never going to do something like this again," Lauren said tightly.

After a moment, Zoe sighed. "O-kay."

CHAPTER 9

The next morning, Lauren woke up with a start. She'd tossed and turned all night, dreaming of a silent alarm. But no one – including the police – had hammered on the door in the middle of the night, demanding to know why they'd been in Paula's house.

Thoughts of being arrested preyed on her mind all morning. Not even the sight of the lavender cupcakes in the glass case, with their shiny fondant icing and purple sprigs, could lift her mood.

"What's up?" Zoe asked her just before lunch.

"*You know*," Lauren whispered. It hadn't been too busy, although their customers had oohed and ahhed over her latest creation. Luckily, she'd kept three aside for her, Zoe, and Ed, although she didn't even feel like eating hers.

"Mitch? Jeff killing Paula?" Zoe appeared deep in thought. "What should we have for dinner tonight?"

"Paula's house." Luckily, the only customers were near the back of the room. Annie was curled up in her bed, dozing.

"Oh, that." Zoe waved her hand in the air. "We're safe, don't worry."

"How do you know that?"

"We haven't been arrested. Even if there had been a silent alarm, there weren't any police around."

"Unless you count Mitch."

"And he doesn't even know what we did." Zoe gave her a sideways glance. "Unless you told him?"

"No! When would I have time to do that? Not that I did."

"After you went to bed. You could have called him to confess."

"Well, I didn't." Lauren frowned at her cousin.

"Good. We're in the clear."

"I thought you said it would be no big deal – and I didn't see any plants in Paula's house to water – did you?"

"No," Zoe confessed. "Never mind. I was wrong. It *was* a bigger deal than I thought it would be. And you were right to say we shouldn't do something like that again."

"I think my exact words were, *'We are never going to do something like this again.' "*. Lauren gave Zoe a schoolmarm look.

"Yes, Mom. But now we know that Jeff had a good motive for killing Paula. Years of built up resentment toward the woman who tricked him – or seduced him – into marriage. He's left with practically nothing after the divorce—"

"He kept his flower shop."

"So, BAM! He strangles Paula with a hair dryer."

"Where did he get the hair dryer from?" Lauren asked.

"He probably bought it."

"And how many years were they married?"

"I don't know." Zoe gave Lauren an exasperated look. "I'm building a scenario here. I don't have quite all the answers yet."

"We have to find out if they were childless," Lauren reminded her.

"That's right." Zoe nodded. "Ooh, I bet Mrs. Finch would know. She knows practically everyone in town because she's lived here so long. And it's club night tomorrow night!"

"How are you going to practice pottery

in Mrs. Finch's living room?" Lauren asked.

"Hmm. I haven't thought that far ahead," Zoe admitted. "I'll read up on it first, because I think it would be awesome to use a potter's wheel and make vases and stuff like that."

"Don't you need to put them in a special oven at a high temperature?"

"Yeah. Maybe there are pottery classes somewhere – there should be in Sacramento."

"And maybe you can get together with Chris while you're there," Lauren teased. She felt guilty when Zoe's expression dimmed.

"Well, he did text me while you had a cold, but I told him I was too busy then," she said.

"I'm sorry," Lauren said. "I would have been fine if you'd wanted to go on a date."

"I know, but I would have felt mean enjoying myself while you were sick," Zoe explained. "I guess I could text him back and suggest a movie we could see."

"Good idea." Lauren smiled.

Zoe picked up her phone, her fingers

busy on the keypad. "It's all set," she announced a few minutes later. "Saturday night."

"I'm going out with Mitch then," Lauren told her.

"And I'm going out with Chris!"

***

"It's club night, Annie," Lauren told the silver-gray tabby Friday afternoon. The last customer had just left, and she decided to close a few minutes early.

"Brrt!" Annie jumped down from her bed and trotted to the private hallway leading to the cottage.

"We have to clean up first." Zoe mock-pouted. "Then have dinner, and *then* go to Mrs. Finch's."

"Brrt!"

Lauren and Zoe cleaned up as quickly as they could. Lauren now felt back to normal again – no sign of her cold returning, thank goodness. And she hadn't infected Zoe or Mitch.

After a quick dinner of beef stew that she'd made yesterday, the trio left for Mrs. Finch's.

"Wait until I tell her I'm thinking of exploring pottery." Zoe giggled as they jumped into Lauren's car. It was too chilly to walk the short distance, and Lauren didn't want Annie's paws to get cold on the sidewalk.

"I'm going to work on my hat," Lauren declared as they pulled up outside Mrs. Finch's house. "I didn't make much progress when I had my cold."

"Maybe you'll finish it tonight," Zoe suggested, getting out of the car.

"Maybe." Lauren didn't want to be overly optimistic. It had already taken her longer than she'd thought.

Mrs. Finch greeted them, ushering them inside.

"I hope you didn't catch a chill outside," she worried as they followed her down the lilac hallway to the fawn and beige living room.

"We've got lots of layers on," Zoe told her, shrugging off her coat.

"We were only outside for a few seconds." Lauren smiled at the senior.

"Brrt!" Annie agreed.

"And Annie should be well equipped for the cold – her ancestors came from

Norway," Lauren added.

Once they were settled on the sofa, Lauren pulled out her knitting. *Click, clack.* She found the sound soothing as she started on the next round of her hat.

Zoe told Mrs. Finch about her pottery idea, while Annie visited them all in turn, spending extra time with Mrs. Finch. They admired Mrs. Finch's hair, which looked neat and tidy in its usual bun, and she told them how pleased she'd been with Brooke's hairdressing skills.

"What have you girls been up to this week?" their hostess asked. "Do you have any news about who killed Paula?"

"We were going to ask you about that," Zoe said. "Do you know if Paula and Jeff had kids?"

"No." Mrs. Finch shook her head. "I only knew her slightly – although I was on better terms with her parents before they moved overseas – but I never heard that she'd had a child."

"Hmm," Zoe murmured.

"Why did you want to know?" Mrs. Finch asked.

"Just a theory we had," Lauren told her. "We heard that Paula and Jeff's divorce was acrimonious and we wondered if there were children involved."

"Yes, I heard about their divorce." Mrs. Finch tsked. "Such a shame. Jeff is a nice young man and deserves a nice young lady. I don't think Paula was the one for him."

"Really?" Zoe exchanged a glance with Lauren.

"I think Paula was looking for a husband just so she could say she was married," Mrs. Finch mused. "Her friend Helen has been married for years, and I think Paula might have felt a bit left out."

"Anything else?" Zoe asked eagerly.

"Well, there was that spot of bother with Helen's husband," Mrs. Finch replied.

"What sort of bother?" Lauren put her knitting aside.

"Brrt?" Annie added.

"Oh, it didn't amount to much," Mrs. Finch told them. "But I was there, so I saw it all."

"Ooh, what did you see?" Zoe stared at her with wide eyes.

"There was a little Christmas party a

couple of years ago. Helen hosted it, and invited me as we used to play cards with a few other ladies – it was a regular activity until everyone became too busy," Mrs. Finch said sadly. "Anyway, Helen invited me to her party. She also invited Paula. I don't know why she wanted to be friends with her, really."

"What happened?" Zoe asked.

"Paula and Jeff had broken up and had started divorce proceedings. Paula seemed very bitter about the relationship ending, and made a play for Helen's husband."

"No way!" Zoe's mouth parted.

"Helen saw what was happening and pulled Paula aside. Paula got upset and left in a huff."

"What about Helen's husband?" Lauren asked. "What did he do?"

"Tried to fend her off as far as I could tell," Mrs. Finch answered. "I don't think he ever liked Paula."

"And Helen and Paula remained friends?" Zoe crinkled her brow.

"It looks like that," Mrs. Finch replied. "I used to see them together sometimes when I was doing my shopping. You'd never know that something like that had happened between them."

"I don't know if I could remain friends with someone who tried to steal my husband," Zoe said.

"Me neither," Lauren agreed. How would she feel if someone she knew made a pass at Mitch? Not happy, that's for sure.

Lauren and Zoe made coffee using Mrs. Finch's pod machine. Lauren kept working on her hat afterward, until they said goodnight to their hostess and made their way home.

"I still think Jeff could be the killer," Zoe remarked as Lauren drove them home.

"Even though he has an alibi?"

"He already lied about it once. What if he lied again?"

CHAPTER 10

The next morning, Lauren and Zoe discussed Jeff's alibi – delivering Baxley, the dog from the shelter, to Rhonda's house as a surprise for her husband's birthday.

"But surely the police would have checked it all out by now," Lauren told Zoe as she steamed milk for a mocha. The café was half full that morning. "Do you really think Jeff would have lied to the police? Didn't Rhonda say the police knew the truth?"

"He lied to *us*, didn't he?" Zoe looked up from plating a lavender cupcake.

"But we're not the police."

Zoe grumbled something Lauren couldn't quite catch. It sounded suspiciously like, "*Almost* the police."

Annie tended to the customers, leading them to the tables, sitting with her favorites for a while, and at other times, having a quick doze in her bed.

Lauren understood why Zoe was so gung-ho about Jeff being the prime suspect, but why would he kill his ex-wife? Surely, if he were a murderer, he would have done the deed during the divorce – or perhaps just before he and Paula separated? Depending on Paula's will, if he had killed her back then, he might have inherited everything she had owned, if she hadn't gotten around to changing it.

With a sigh, Lauren resolved not to think about Paula's death any more that day. They closed at lunch time on Saturdays, which meant she'd have a few hours to relax before getting ready for her date with Mitch that evening.

A couple of hours later, their last customer departed and Zoe bolted the front door.

"Now all we have to do is clean up and have the rest of the weekend to ourselves."

"Brrt!" Annie agreed, jumping out of her bed and running to the door leading to the private hallway.

"Do you want to go home already, Annie?" Lauren laughed as she unlocked the door. "There you go."

"Brrp." Annie ran down the hallway and shimmied through the cat flap, landing in the cottage kitchen.

"I wish I could do that." Zoe grinned.

They quickly cleaned and tidied the café, then ate lunch in the cottage. Zoe had saved paninis for them, as well as a lavender cupcake each.

"What am I going to wear tonight?" Zoe tapped her cheek after finishing her meal.

"Where are you going with Chris?" Lauren asked curiously.

"To the movie theater in Zeke's Ridge. There's a chick flick I want to see, and he said I could choose."

"Let me know if it's any good."

"I will. If I love it, then I won't mind seeing it again, and we can watch it together one day."

"Sounds like a plan." Lauren smiled.

After lunch, Zoe riffled through her outfits.

"We're also having dinner," she said in a muffled voice, her head stuck inside the closet.

"Brrp?" Annie jumped onto Zoe's bed, kneading the purple bedspread.

"We're helping Zoe find something to wear for her date with Chris tonight," Lauren explained.

Zoe flung a few pieces of clothing onto the bed: a black miniskirt, black skinny jeans, white slacks, a red dress.

"Too cold, too casual, too dressy, too clingy." Zoe pointed to each item.

"What else do you have?" Lauren asked.

"This. And this. And this." Zoe pulled out more clothes from the closet.

"Brrt!" Annie jumped onto the red tunic Zoe tossed onto the bed.

"This one?" Zoe fingered it. "What about these black leggings to go with it, Annie?" She pulled them out of a dresser drawer and held them up.

"Brrt," Annie said encouragingly.

"I think Annie wants you to wear that outfit," Lauren said. "I think it suits you."

"Well, if you both agree …" Zoe nodded. "Okay."

"Brrt." Annie approved.

"Now we've decided on my outfit, what will Lauren wear, Annie?" Zoe asked.

"I'm going to wear my teal dress, and the necklace Mitch gave me." Lauren touched the piece of jewelry.

"Good choice." Zoe nodded.

Zoe took a shower and got ready. She'd just fixed her hair when the doorbell rang.

"He's here!" Zoe looked panicked for a second.

"Annie and I will let him in." Lauren headed toward the front door, Annie running ahead of her.

"Hi," she greeted Chris as she opened the door. He wore black slacks and a navy sweater. "Zoe will be ready in a second."

"Brrt," Annie added.

"Hi, Lauren. Hi, Annie." He bent down to talk to the feline.

"I'm ready." Zoe's voice sounded from behind Lauren.

"You look great." Chris studied Zoe. Pink tinged her cheeks.

"So do you," she murmured.

Lauren hid a smile. Her cousin and Chris seemed equally smitten with each other, although she thought they were both trying to keep their attraction to each other low key.

"Let's go," Zoe said briskly.

"Bye." Lauren waved to them.

Once they'd left, Lauren turned to

Annie. "What are you going to do tonight? You'll be in charge of the cottage."

"Brrt!" Annie agreed. She trotted toward Lauren's bedroom.

"Now it's my turn to get ready," Lauren told the feline as she pulled her outfit out of the closet.

Taking a quick shower, she slipped on her dress and blow-dried her hair. As she glanced at the cord plugged into the wall socket, she was transported to the moment she saw Paula's dead body, her spine prickling.

She shook off the disturbing thought and concentrated on getting ready. Annie sat on the bed, watching her every move.

"Do you want me to leave the TV on for you tonight?" Lauren asked.

"Brrt." *Yes.*

Lauren finished getting ready, the doorbell chiming just as she checked her appearance.

"Want to say hello to Mitch?" Lauren asked Annie, who reclined on the bed.

"Brrp," Annie said agreeably, jumping down and scampering to the front door.

"Hi," Lauren said as she opened the

door, noticing he wore the scarf she'd knitted for him. The fawn color complimented his gray jacket and slacks.

"Hi," Mitch replied, his dark brown eyes warm as he surveyed her.

"Brrt!" Annie interrupted the little moment of silence.

"Hi, Annie." He crouched a little and smiled at the cat.

"I'll be home later," Lauren told her.

"Brrp." *I know.*

Lauren locked the door behind her, thinking it was a little strange that both she and Zoe were out on a Saturday night, and Annie was the only one at home. She hoped Annie wouldn't miss her – or Zoe. Maybe Annie would enjoy a little time on her own to relax in the cottage.

Mitch drove them to their favorite bistro on the outskirts of Gold Leaf Valley. They told each other what they'd been up to that week; Mitch was still working extra shifts, and Lauren told him the lavender cupcakes had proven popular. However, she didn't mention the night he had discovered her and Zoe near Paula's house.

Should she say anything about it to him? She finally decided, no, she wouldn't – not unless he asked her. She felt guilty reaching that decision, but realized she didn't want to put Mitch in an awkward predicament by telling him that she and Zoe had entered Paula's house without permission – even if they had found a spare key.

The bistro was moderately busy, the murmur of other diners providing a backdrop to their conversation. This time, Lauren decided to be adventurous and order something different to pork with four varieties of apples, and chose the braised beef with mushrooms, while Mitch ordered the pan roasted salmon.

To Lauren's relief, nobody sneezed on her this time – and there weren't any diners coughing, either.

"Maybe we should have come here last time," Mitch spoke as they waited for their dessert of molten chocolate brownie with vanilla bean ice cream.

Lauren smiled, wondering if she should be surprised or not that he'd practically read her mind. The only area that they seemed to disagree on was her and Zoe's sleuthing attempts, although Mitch now seemed to realize that he needed to accept Lauren's involvement in such matters, however much he disliked it.

They lingered over coffee after their dessert. Mitch invited her to lunch at a local winery the following day, and Lauren accepted with pleasure.

Mitch pulled up outside her cottage. Lauren had left the porch light on when she'd departed.

"I wonder if Zoe is back from her date with Chris," she mused. "They were going to see a movie at Zeke's Ridge and have dinner."

"Chris told me about that." Mitch smiled. "He said Zoe's different to any other girl he's met."

"I think they're a good match." Lauren turned to him. "Don't you?"

"Yes." Mitch traced his finger along her cheek. "And I think we're a good match, too."

CHAPTER 11

Zoe hummed as she slathered butter onto her toast the next morning.

"That movie was great last night," she enthused. "We should have a girls' night out and go see it, and have dinner after. Chris and I went to that Italian restaurant that you and Mitch have been to, and the meatballs were delish."

"Yes, they do have good food there," Lauren agreed. "Pick a time and we'll go."

"Brrt!" Annie said.

"They don't let cats into the movie theater," Lauren told her. "I'm sorry."

"Brrp," Annie grumbled, then turned around on the kitchen chair next to Lauren's and curled up in a circle, nose to tail.

"Maybe Annie stayed up all night watching TV." Zoe grinned.

"Maybe." Lauren stroked the silver-gray tabby, the fur soft as velvet beneath her fingertips.

"Did you guys have a good time last night?" Zoe asked.

"Yes." She told her cousin about the

previous evening, and Mitch's invitation to the winery today.

"It looks like you and me today, Annie." Zoe winked at the cat.

"Brrt." Annie sounded a little sleepy.

After breakfast, Lauren got ready for her date with Mitch. Annie watched her every move, sighing when Lauren waved goodbye to her at the front door.

"I promise we'll have special TV time tonight," Lauren told her.

"Brrt!" Annie brightened.

On her date, Lauren ended up buying a bottle of delightful Zinfandel, while Mitch bought a bottle of award-winning Pinot Noir. They enjoyed a simple lunch of freshly baked bread, cheese, and a green salad at the winery café.

They made plans to have dinner the following Thursday, Lauren wondering if she would finish knitting her hat by then. Maybe she could wear it if they weren't going anywhere too fancy.

She spent the evening with Annie and Zoe on the sofa, watching TV, Annie curled up in her lap, all thoughts of the murder in a distant corner of her mind.

***

On Tuesday, Lauren and Zoe opened the café on the dot of nine-thirty. They'd spent Monday doing housework, grocery shopping, and checking on Mrs. Finch. The senior assured them she was fine and planned to visit the café the following day.

"When are you seeing Chris again?" Lauren asked Zoe as they stood behind the counter, ready for their first customer.

"Next Saturday," Zoe told her. "Although this time we might do something in Sacramento, like bowling or mini-golf."

"That sounds fun."

"Hey, maybe you and Mitch can double with us!"

Lauren stared at her cousin. The idea had merit.

"I'll talk to Mitch about it."

The faint banging of tins in the kitchen signaled Ed hard at work making his pastries.

A couple of customers came in, having problems deciding between a blueberry Danish or a triple chocolate ganache cupcake.

Helen walked into the café. Annie trotted to greet her at the *Please Wait to be Seated* sign.

"What a pretty girl you are."

"Brrt," Annie agreed, before leading her to a small table in the middle of the room.

Lauren and Zoe watched Helen peruse the small menu, then scrape her wooden chair back and walk over to the counter to order.

"What can we get you?" Lauren asked.

"Ooh, that *is* my bracelet." Zoe pointed to the pink and turquoise beads decorating Helen's wrist.

"This? I love it." Helen patted the bangle, her hand resting on it. "My husband bought it for me as a little surprise. He's always so thoughtful."

"I thought I saw you wear it when we were at the salon," Zoe said. "You know, when—" she lowered her voice "— Paula complained about her perm."

"Yes, I wear it nearly all the time," Helen said. "My hubby told me he bought it from here, but I don't see any for sale now."

"That's because it was the only one that sold." Zoe sounded disappointed. "So I decided only to make them for friends and family – and myself, of course." She pointed to the gold beads around her wrist.

"What a shame," Helen sympathized. "If you decide to make them again to sell, please let me know."

"Will do." Zoe cheered up.

Lauren made the large latte while Zoe plated the apricot Danish for Helen.

They left Helen to enjoy her order, while Annie checked on the other customers, hopping up onto a vacant chair at each table, and after a moment, hopping down.

"I wonder when Mrs. Finch will get here." Zoe furrowed her brow.

"Soon, I hope," Lauren replied.

A few minutes later, Annie ran to the *Please Wait to be Seated* sign.

"Brrt!" she greeted one of her favorite customers.

"Hi, Mrs. Finch," Zoe called out.

"Hello, dears." Mrs. Finch beamed at them. Today she wore a beige skirt with a dusty rose blouse, and a heavy navy coat.

Lauren watched Mrs. Finch follow Annie to a small table near the counter and sink down into the pine chair.

"Let's go over." She nudged Zoe.

"What can we get you?" Zoe asked as they approached.

"Brrt," Annie answered, sitting opposite the senior.

"I would love a cup of tea today, girls," Mrs. Finch replied. "And one of your lavender cupcakes, if you have any, Lauren."

"Yes, we do." Lauren smiled.

"Do you have an update on – you know." Mrs. Finch lowered her voice. "I see Helen is here."

"Yes, she is, but no, we don't know anything else," Zoe told her. "Unfortunately."

"I'm sure you two will work it out. You always do."

"You're right. We do!" Zoe grinned.

Lauren wondered if it was sometimes the case of being in the right place at the right time – or the wrong time, when they'd found themselves confronting a killer. But she didn't want to burst Zoe's sleuthing bubble.

They brought Mrs. Finch's order over to her, and chatted with her for a few minutes. More customers came in, so they made their apologies and tended to the newcomers.

The rest of the day was busy, and Lauren only had time to catch her breath at four o'clock, when the café was finally empty.

"Phew!" Zoe flopped onto a stool behind the counter.

"I know." Lauren wiggled her feet as she sat next to her cousin.

"Brrt." Annie patted something on the floor near her bed. She pushed it with her paw, a little turquoise ball that skated along the floor to the other side of the café. She ran after it, pouncing on it.

"What have you got there?" Lauren jumped down from the stool and hurried over to the silver-gray tabby.

"Brrt." Annie pushed the bead toward Lauren.

"Have you lost a bead from your bracelet?" she called out to Zoe.

Zoe looked down at her wrist. "No."

"Your bangle has gold balls on it today, hasn't it?"

"That's right." Zoe came over to them and looked at the bead in Lauren's hand. "Helen wore a bangle with this color bead, though. It was the two-tone one I made, turquoise and pink. Remember I thought I saw it on her wrist at the salon when Brooke trimmed your hair?"

"That's right." Lauren nodded. Something tickled in the back of her mind. She drew in a deep breath. "Did you say that Helen's bracelet also has *pink* beads on it?"

"Yep. I really like that color combination."

"I saw a speck of pink at the murder scene," Lauren said slowly. "Like a small bead."

"Like this bead?" Zoe tapped the turquoise ball.

"Yes. But pink."

"It can't be Helen." Zoe's eyes widened. "I thought we liked Jeff for the murderer."

"She just said she wears that bracelet a lot," Lauren told her. "And this bead came off it today, because it definitely wasn't lying on the floor when we opened this morning. What if a bead fell off it at the murder scene?"

"Why are beads dropping off the bracelet I made?" Zoe frowned. "Didn't I attach them properly?" She looked downcast. After a second, she snapped back to attention. "But why would she kill her friend?"

"Because Paula wasn't such a good friend to her, if she made a pass at Helen's husband."

"But that happened a couple of years ago," Zoe protested.

"I didn't notice Jeff wearing a pink bracelet when he came in last, did you?" Lauren asked.

"And he hasn't been in here today," Zoe conceded.

They looked at each other for a moment, then spoke at the same time.

"Helen must be the killer!"

CHAPTER 12

"I'm going to call Mitch." Lauren pulled out her phone. Luckily, nobody had entered the café since they'd found the bead.

"Brrt?" Annie asked. She'd been silent since she'd shown Lauren her trophy.

"It's Annie's Lost and Found again," Zoe marveled, "except this time she's found a clue."

"Brrt!" *That's right!*

"Shouldn't we call the detective who's handling the case?" Zoe countered. "It'll be quicker."

"Good idea."

Zoe dug out her phone from her jeans' pocket and dialed. "He gave me his card when he interviewed me, and I added his number," she explained to Lauren. "Just in case."

She nodded, watching her cousin frown as she listened on her cell.

"Yuck. I have to leave a message." Zoe quickly explained their theory of Helen being the killer and ended the call. "I hope he takes us seriously."

"So do I."

"Brrt!"

Lauren was on tenterhooks for the next hour, wondering if Helen was suddenly going to burst in and confront them, but as five o'clock came and went, she slowly relaxed. Since it had been quiet, she and Zoe had gotten a head start on the cleaning and now there was very little to do.

"Maybe she's not the murderer." Lauren locked the big oak door, shooting the bolt across.

"Who else could it be?" Zoe stacked chairs on the tables. "If it's not Jeff, and it sounds like he had plenty of motive to kill his ex-wife, then who?"

"Helen's husband?" Lauren guessed. "Maybe he didn't like being in the middle between his wife and Paula."

"Ooh, that's a good theory," Zoe praised. "Except why would he wait until now to kill Paula?"

"We should think about that while we finish tidying up."

"Yes, boss." Zoe grinned.

It didn't take long for them to ready the café for the next morning.

"I want to check on the herb garden,"

Lauren said. "Let's go out through the kitchen today."

"Okay."

Lauren opened the private hallway for Annie, who scampered toward the cat flap leading to the cottage. She wondered if Annie would then shimmy through the other flap attached to the back door to the cottage, which led to the rear garden.

Zoe followed Lauren through the gleaming commercial kitchen, and out the back door where the herb garden was situated.

"Brrt!" Annie sat near the herbs, looking like she'd been waiting for them *forever.*

"I've just had a genius idea!" Zoe's expression looked impish. "Why don't we set a trap for Helen? And then we'll know for sure if she's guilty."

"How?" Lauren asked.

"We'll tell her we've found a pink bead and ask if she lost one from her bracelet. And we'll also tell her we picked up another pink bead from outside the salon – we don't have to mention it was when we found Paula's body," Zoe added hurriedly.

"No, that's too dangerous," Lauren said. "If we can't get hold of the detective who interviewed you, then we should call Mitch. Even if we have to leave a message, he might get back to us faster than the other detective."

"O-kay," Zoe grumbled. "But I bet my idea will get us faster results."

"Your idea might get us killed."

"How right you are, Lauren." Helen came into view from around the side of the building.

Zoe sent Lauren a desperate *Eeek!* glance.

"What are you doing here, Helen?" Lauren faked furrowing her brow. She didn't think it worked.

"I realized just now that that I'd lost another bead from that darn bracelet. The only place I visited today was your café. So I came back to see if anyone had found it, but you were closed. I knocked on the door and there was no answer, so I thought I'd try around the back. I know your kitchen's here." She pointed to the back door they'd just exited – and locked.

"Here's your bead." Lauren held it out to her, not caring they were giving away evidence. She only wanted the three of them to get away safely.

"Thanks." Helen snatched it and shoved it into her purse. "I was worried you'd noticed today a bead was missing – that must have been the one I'd dropped when I placed Paula's body outside the salon. That's why I covered it with my hand when you admired it today."

"And I thought you were patting your bracelet because you liked it so much." Zoe looked put out. "It's one of my best pieces."

"I'd stopped wearing the bracelet after I noticed a bead was missing after Paula's – death. But then I thought that might look suspicious, so I started wearing it again."

"Huh," Zoe muttered.

"I'm afraid I heard everything you said just now." Helen looked around the garden, scanning the tidy lawn and the occasional bush. "It's a shame there's not a hair dryer handy – two, actually. I suppose I'll just have to make do with my bare hands."

Lauren, Zoe, and Annie all took a step back.

"But why?" Lauren asked desperately. "I thought Paula was your friend."

"She was," Helen replied. "But she pushed me too far. It was bad enough she made a pass at my husband a couple of years ago. She apologized later and said it was the alcohol talking, and how awful she was feeling about her marriage breaking up. And like an idiot, I believed her and I forgave her. But not this time."

Lauren and Zoe exchanged worried glances.

"What did she do?" Zoe asked.

"She stole my quilting patterns."

"Huh?" Zoe wrinkled her nose.

"My original quilting patterns. I won first prize at the county fair with the quilt I designed myself. I *loved* quilting and coming up with new ideas. But it can be expensive. My husband started criticizing my spending and saying we couldn't afford to spend so much on my hobby, so I gave it up for a while."

"Couldn't you have sold your patterns to make some extra money?" Lauren asked.

"I didn't think anyone would buy them," Helen explained. "The quilting groups I was involved in all kept saying, why should we pay for patterns when there are so many free ones online and in books? I didn't think it would be viable, so I kept my patterns just for myself."

"So how did Paula get her hands on them?" Zoe asked.

"Brrt!" *Exactly!*

"Stupid me believed her when she said she wanted to give quilting a try, but didn't like any of the patterns she'd seen online. She said she loved the quilts I'd designed and wanted to make them for herself. So I gave her copies of my patterns, and photos of the finished quilts."

"Did she make them?" Lauren asked.

"No." Helen shook her head. "She kept saying she was just about to start, and I told her I'd be happy to help her whenever she needed it, but she never asked for my assistance." Helen sounded sad.

"Why were you friends in the first place?" Zoe asked curiously.

"I felt a little sorry for her. She didn't seem to have a best friend and I thought that would be all she needed to show everyone what a good person she was deep down."

"*Very* deep down," Zoe muttered.

"But I was wrong," Helen concluded. "She took advantage of me, and also of other people. She borrowed Rhonda's expensive hair dryer and didn't give it back." She barked with laughter. "I thought it fitting that I used my old hair dryer to strangle her."

"Um, about that," Lauren began.

"I didn't want to." Tears welled in Helen's eyes. "You have no idea how awful I felt about it. A rage just came over me when I found out she'd been passing off my quilt patterns as her own and pocketing the money. *I* could have used that extra cash."

"How did you find out?" Zoe asked.

"That day in the café when Rhonda told me her daughter had seen one of my patterns for sale online. When I got home, I searched online for my work, and she was right! My quilting patterns were for sale, along with the photos I'd given Paula of my finished work.

"I confronted Paula, and you know what she did? She laughed in my face!

181

Said I'd been stupid not to make money from my craft. She told me she didn't think I'd ever find out, as I don't buy patterns. And she was worried at first when I told her I was taking up quilting again, but said she didn't think I was smart enough to discover what she'd been up to."

"I guess you showed her," Zoe uttered.

"Zoe!" Lauren hissed. She didn't want them to make Helen even more murderous.

"But why did you place Paula's body outside Brooke's hair salon?" Zoe asked.

"To place suspicion on Brooke. I felt guilty about that, but since I strangled Paula with the hair dryer cord, I thought it would be a good idea to dump her body there."

"How did you even manage it?" Lauren asked, fascinated despite herself.

"I went to Paula's house early one morning. I was going to ask to borrow her hair dryer, which isn't even hers, it's Rhonda's. I'd found out the night before that she was profiting from my quilting patterns – the sales listings even had a photo of her on it!"

"Wow," Zoe murmured.

"During the drive to her house, I wondered if I'd be able to forgive her if she really was sorry. But she wasn't. And that justified my decision to kill her. I'd brought my own hair dryer and hid it in my big purse when I entered her house. All I had to do was stand behind her, pull out my hair dryer, and wrap the cord around her neck."

The trio took another step back.

"And now you know too much. Lucky for me, the detective hasn't returned your call. Don't you just hate that?"

Helen lunged at them.

Lauren and Zoe shrieked.

"Run!" Lauren made a beeline for the cottage.

Annie raced ahead of her, aiming for the large cat flap in the back door.

Lauren looked behind her.

Zoe yanked her bracelet off and flung it at Helen's face.

"Ow!" Helen placed a hand over her cheek. "You could have gotten my eye!"

Lauren skidded to a stop, pulled off her shoes and hurled them at Helen.

"Ouch!" Helen clutched her head.

"Stop throwing things at me!"

"Stop trying to kill us!" Zoe yelled.

"Brrt!" Annie demanded Lauren's attention. She wriggled through the cat flap, turned around, and stuck her face into it from the cottage kitchen. *"Brrt!"*

Lauren glanced back. Helen advanced toward them, her face battered and red.

Tugging the zipper on her pants pocket to grab the key for the back door, Lauren froze. The zip was stuck. *She had no way of unlocking the back door.*

"Brrt!" Annie's tone was urgent.

Looking into Annie's eyes, Lauren realized what the feline was trying to tell her.

"You want me to crawl through the cat flap?" She shook her head. "I'll never fit." She dug out her phone and pressed 911 with shaking fingers. "Zoe, climb through the flap!" At least she and Annie would be safe in the cottage.

"Here goes – oomph!" Zoe rushed past. Her slim body looked like a wriggling eel as she pulled herself through the cat door. "I'm going to be one big bruise tomorrow." She pulled out her phone. "I'm calling 911 right now!"

"And I'm already calling," Lauren shouted to Helen. The other woman stopped two yards away, suddenly looking uncertain. "Even if you kill me, you can't get to Zoe and Annie. The door is locked and you'll never get through the flap." A voice came on the other end of the phone and Lauren's voice broke as she gave her address and told the operator she was fending off a killer.

"You can too get through here, Lauren." Zoe's voice was fierce as she poked her head through the cat flap. "Come on! Annie and I will help you. We're not leaving you out there."

Lauren crouched down, keeping a wary eye on Helen, who hadn't moved. She knew the other woman was too big for the cat door, but could Lauren fit her curves through it?

She pushed her head and arm through the flap, wiggling and turning her shoulder, until the top half of her was inside the kitchen.

"Brrt!" Annie approved.

"It's not fair!" Helen suddenly wailed. "Why did Paula have to steal my quilting patterns?"

"What's she doing?" Lauren whispered. She couldn't contort her body to look behind her.

"Helen's sitting on the grass and crying." Zoe kept her voice low. "You're nearly inside." Zoe pulled on Lauren's shoulder.

"Ouch!" She sucked in her stomach and wriggled until she thought she could get a job as a contortionist.

"Brrt!" Annie peeped at the side of Lauren's face touching the ground as she slid into the kitchen. "Brrt!" *See?*

"You were right, Annie," Lauren gasped. "I did fit in the cat flap." She lay on the cold kitchen floor wondering if she'd ever be able to get up.

A uniformed officer suddenly appeared on the other side of the back door, bending down to peek at them through the flap.

"Is she the killer?" He pointed to Helen, still sitting on the grass, and sobbing.

EPILOGUE

"I can't believe it was Helen." Zoe shook her head. It was the following day and they'd opened the café on time. Ed was busy making pastries in the kitchen.

"I know," Lauren replied.

"Brrt!"

Annie strolled past the empty tables, as if checking everything was in place for their first customer.

"I'm just glad we found out who the killer was," Zoe continued. "Although, I don't think I'll look at a hair dryer in the same way again."

"Me either."

After Helen had been taken into custody, Mitch had checked on Lauren, making sure she was okay. She wasn't sure if he'd said something to his friend Chris, but Zoe had received a phone call from him, and had been in a good mood after their conversation.

"Our first customers." Zoe bounced on her toes.

"Hi, guys." Brooke and Jeff stood at the *Please Wait to be Seated* sign.

"Brrt." Annie trotted over to them.

"Isn't the salon open today?" Zoe asked.

Brooke flushed. "I don't have any customers booked until later this morning, so I thought I'd play hooky and open a little later."

"I guess I'm a bad influence on you." Jeff gazed warmly at her before turning to Lauren and Zoe. "It was my idea."

"Brrt." *Follow me.* Annie led them to a four-seater near the counter.

Lauren watched the couple sit opposite each other and study the small menu.

"I wonder what's going on there?" Zoe mused.

Annie jumped onto one of the chairs at their table.

"Whatever it is, Annie seems interested." Lauren smiled.

"Let's take their order." Zoe zoomed over to the table. Lauren followed.

"We were just about to come over to the counter," Brooke protested.

"No need." Lauren pulled out her order pad from her apron pocket. "It's quiet at the moment."

"Did you hear that Helen was the killer?" Zoe asked.

"Yes." Jeff nodded. "A detective told me this morning. Apparently, Helen confessed at the police station, with her lawyer present."

"She seemed like such a nice woman," Brooke murmured.

"She was," Jeff told her. "I always thought Paula was lucky to have a friend like Helen, but I was wrong. Helen was *unlucky* to have Paula as a friend."

All five of them were silent for a moment.

"Brrp," Annie encouraged.

"I think she wants you to order," Lauren said.

"Brrt." *Yes.*

They both ordered large lattes, with a lavender cupcake each to go.

"I wonder if they're dating," Zoe murmured to Lauren as she placed the cupcakes into brown paper bags.

"Maybe," Lauren answered, glancing up from the milk wand to see Brooke touch her hair as she gazed at Jeff.

"He certainly seems happy to be here with her." Zoe watched Lauren wiggle the milk jug until a peacock bloomed on the surface of the first latte.

"Mm hm." Lauren made a second peacock.

"I'm going to find out." Zoe grabbed the paper bags and hurried over to the table.

Lauren's eyes widened as she realized what her cousin was up to.

Carrying the lattes on a tray, she reached the table just as she heard Zoe say:

"You two make a cute couple."

Brooke blushed, and Jeff's ears turned pink.

"Here are your lattes." Lauren placed them on the table and gave Zoe a warning look. Which Zoe ignored.

"How long have you been dating?"

Brooke and Jeff looked at each other, as if wondering if the other would speak.

"Not long," Brooke finally said.

"The first time we met was when I delivered flowers to her at the salon. You two were there."

Zoe nodded.

"We're just getting to know each other." Brooke smiled at Jeff.

"Then we'll leave you to it." Lauren picked up the tray.

"Wait!" Jeff pulled out his phone. "Can you take a photo of us? I can't take a good selfie."

Brooke stared at him. "Me either," she confessed.

They both laughed.

"I'd be happy to." Lauren took the phone and stepped back a few paces. "Lean forward so I can get you both in."

Brooke and Jeff inched forward off their chairs so they were leaning across the table, their heads almost touching. Annie stayed where she was, in the seat between them.

"Smile!" Zoe called out, standing off to the side.

Just as Lauren pressed the button …

"Brrt!" Annie jumped from the chair onto the table, her head between Brooke's and Jeff's.

Click!

Lauren stifled a giggle as she looked at the cat standing on the table. Annie seemed very pleased with herself.

"Let me see." Zoe peered over Lauren's shoulder at the photo. "Oh, that's so cute!"

"Do you want me to take another

one?" Lauren handed Jeff the phone.

A grin hovered on his lips. "No, it's good." He gave the phone to Brooke.

"Oh, Annie, I didn't know you were a photobomber." She laughed and showed Annie the image.

"Brrt." Annie inclined her head slightly.

"I think it's perfect," Brooke said.

Lauren and Zoe headed back to the counter.

"I think we should give them some privacy," Lauren whispered.

"Good idea," Zoe whispered back. "Hey." Her eyes widened. "Jeff didn't have that *how did this happen* look on his face just now when you took the photo, like he did in his wedding picture at Paula's house."

"No, he didn't."

Annie jumped off the table and strolled over to the counter, looking up at Lauren and Zoe.

"I think Annie's given Brooke and Jeff her seal of approval, haven't you?" Zoe winked at the silver-gray tabby.

"Don't you mean her *photo* of approval?" Lauren smiled at Annie.

"Brrt!"

THE END

I hope you enjoyed reading this mystery. Sign up to my newsletter at http://www.JintyJames.com and be among the first to discover when my next book is published!

Previous Titles:

Purrs and Peril – A Norwegian Forest Cat Café Cozy Mystery – Book 1

Meow Means Murder – A Norwegian Forest Cat Café Cozy Mystery – Book 2

Whiskers and Warrants – A Norwegian Forest Cat Café Cozy Mystery – Book 3

Two Tailed Trouble – A Norwegian Forest Cat Café Cozy Mystery – Book 4

Maddie Goodwell Series (fun witch cozies)

Spells and Spiced Latte - A Coffee Witch Cozy Mystery - Maddie Goodwell 1
Please note: Spells and Spiced Latte should be free on Amazon. If it's not, please contact me via Facebook (I'm on it nearly every day) or email me at jinty@jintyjames.com

Visions and Vanilla Cappuccino - A Coffee Witch Cozy Mystery - Maddie Goodwell 2

Magic and Mocha – A Coffee Witch Cozy Mystery – Maddie Goodwell 3

Enchantments and Espresso – A Coffee Witch Cozy Mystery – Maddie Goodwell 4

Familiars and French Roast - A Coffee Witch Cozy Mystery – Maddie Goodwell 5

Incantations and Iced Coffee – A Coffee Witch Cozy Mystery – Maddie Goodwell 6

Made in the USA
Monee, IL
29 December 2021

87512614R00121